"What if I get pregnant?"

"Stacie," Cole said, practically begging, his ___ on her shoulders again, "I'll use protection. ___ smart. We'll be safe. Whatever you want me ___ 'll do it, so you won't have to worry about a ___

Stacie looked down at the floor, as if giving it ___ serious thought.

"I love you, baby. Just say yes, and everything ___ be fine."

Stacie looked up at him. "Cole . . ." she began.

"Yes, baby," Cole said, kissing her quickly on the ___. "Anything."

"I can't."

Stacie & Cole

RM JOHNSON

JUMP AT THE SUN

HYPERION

NEW YORK

First Edition

1 3 5 7 9 10 8 6 4 2

Printed in the United States of America

Library of Congress Cataloging-in-Publication Data on file

ISBN-13: 978-14231-0598-5

ISBN-10: 1-4231-0598-2

Visit www.jumpatthesun.com

To my dear nieces, Porsha and Taylor,
and my favorite nephew, Coy.
Be true to what you desire,
and pursue that over all things.

Stacie & Cole

In the beginning . . .

COLE STEPPED into the cafeteria and practically tripped at the sight of her. She was beautiful, with her long black hair, her beautiful, cocoa-brown complexion, her modelesque shape. After two weeks of high school, she was the first girl to make Cole feel truly speechless.

He motioned his friend Marc over to a table near where the girl was sitting. Like Cole, Marc was proudly wearing his varsity-football practice jersey. Cole continued to stare, entranced, at the girl as they set their lunch trays down.

"Why don't you go over there and say hi?" Marc coaxed. "You're the man! You made quarterback as a *freshman*. You can have any chick in this school."

Cole broke his gaze and turned to Marc, a look of incredulity on his face. "Does she look like just any girl to you? What if she blows me off?"

"Then I'm gonna laugh, and talk about you for a week. Just go for it, man," Marc said with a chuckle, giving Cole a friendly slap on the shoulder.

Cole wished he shared his friend's confidence. Slowly, hesitantly, he pushed back from the table, stood up, and made his way over to her.

She was sitting with five other girls and didn't notice Cole's approach until he was practically standing over her. Two of her friends glanced up at Cole, then looked back down and giggled. She turned around and saw Cole smiling shyly at her.

"Uh, hi. My name is Cole," was all he could muster. But as he saw her return his smile and pull out a chair for him, he knew it was enough.

"Hi, Cole. I'm Stacie."

That day, Cole walked Stacie home from school. He was thrilled by how quickly they had opened up to each other, how easy it was to talk to her.

She stopped suddenly when they got to the corner of the street where her house was located.

"Um, sorry. You gotta stop here," she said, looking slightly embarrassed.

"How come? I don't mind walking you to your

door. Oh, you don't want me to see where you live?"

"It's not that. . . . It's just . . . my dad is kinda over-protective. You know what I mean?" Stacie smiled apologetically.

"Yeah." Cole smiled back. "I think I know what you mean."

The two of them stood on the corner, awkwardly avoiding direct eye contact for about thirty seconds, each waiting for the other to make a move.

Finally, Stacie stuck her hand out. "Well, it was nice meeting you. Thanks for walking me home."

"Oh! Yeah, no problem—and ditto," Cole said, slightly disappointed in himself. He wished he had had the nerve to ask for a kiss.

He turned and had started to walk off when he heard Stacie call out to him.

"Hey, Cole?"

He turned back to her. "Stacie?"

"You think we can do this again tomorrow?"

Cole didn't bother trying to hide the huge grin that came over his face. "Uh, okay. Yeah. I think we can do that."

Chapter One

STACIE SAT at the kitchen table, her book bag slung over the back of her chair, a bowl of what had once been sugarcoated cereal sitting in front of her. The spoon was still in her tense grip, but the little bit of milk at the bottom of the bowl had practically dried out.

She wanted to get up, drop the bowl and spoon in the sink, shoulder her book bag, and leave, but she knew she had to wait. She had to face the showdown.

Normally, her father would've been having breakfast with her. It was just the two of them now, so he insisted that they start the day off together, eating and talking about the day ahead.

But this morning was different. He wasn't sitting across from her with his suit and tie on, eating his oatmeal or bran cereal. He was upstairs, probably brooding about what had happened the previous afternoon, just as she had been doing all morning. Just as she was doing right now.

Stacie's father had come home early from work—even for a Sunday—at exactly 1:37 p.m. She knew what time it was because she'd been lying on the living room sofa when it happened, her head turned to the side, absentmindedly staring at the clock on the VCR.

The only problem was, when her father walked through the front door and stepped into the living room, Stacie wasn't alone on the sofa.

Her boyfriend, Cole, was lying on top of her, his tongue making circles in her ear.

The two teenagers scrambled to react as Stacie's father's briefcase fell from his hand and crashed to the hardwood floor.

Cole immediately slid off the couch and then tried as quickly as he could to get up off the floor.

Stacie sat up, yanked the front of her T-shirt down to cover her exposed bra, grateful that she hadn't taken the shirt off altogether, and looked fearfully at her father, who was still standing just inside the doorway, an expression of shock and horror on his face.

He didn't speak a word at first, just looked Stacie and

Cole over with disgust. He opened his mouth a couple of times, looking as though he were trying to form words—but they would not come.

Then, all of a sudden, he sprang to life, taking several long, quick strides across the room, grabbing Cole by his arm, and dragging him toward the door.

"Mr. Winston, I—" Cole didn't even get to finish his sentence.

"Daddy, no!" Stacie said, jumping up from the sofa. "Please! It's not what it looks like."

Her father stopped, his hand still firmly around Cole's arm.

"Then what were you two doing?"

"We were—"

"No, that was a stupid question. I know exactly what he was here for. Now, come on," Stacie's father said, giving Cole's arm a firm yank. He swung the door open, led Cole out, and tried to pull the door closed behind them, but Stacie rushed over and positioned herself in the doorway.

"Where are you taking him?" she asked.

"Stay in the house, Stacie. Stay!"

Gently but firmly, her father pushed her out of the way and closed the door. Stacie ran to the front windows to try to see where her father was taking Cole. She saw them approach the sidewalk, where her father stopped and stood face to face with Cole. Stacie couldn't make out what her father was saying, but she was sure she could guess. He kept pointing his finger at Cole's face, then back toward the house, then back at Cole. When his diatribe was over, he stared stone-faced at Cole, his arms folded across his chest. Then Cole began to walk slowly away, his head hung low.

Stacie waited for what seemed like an eternity for her father to walk back into the house.

"What did you tell him?" Stacie asked, on the verge of tears.

"Go to your room, Stacie," her father said, his voice surprisingly calm.

"Daddy, why did you have to grab him like that? All we were doing was—"

"I know what he was doing!" Her father's voice had an edge to it. "Now, go to your room, Stacie. Please."

She did as she was told—not that she had much choice. She figured that when her dad was ready, he'd eventually knock softly on her door and tell her it was time to talk about what happened. But the knock never came.

"Good morning, sweetheart."

At the breakfast table, Stacie jumped, nearly dropping her spoon in surprise, as she realized that her father was standing just inside the kitchen doorway. She tried to read his face for clues, but she had no idea what he was thinking.

"I've made you late for school, so I'll drive you today."

"Dad, you don't—"

"I'm driving you," he insisted.

He stepped closer, pulled out a chair, then started to speak haltingly, as if testing the right combination of words in his head before saying them aloud. "I—I'm sorry I handled Cole the way I did. I didn't mean to be so rough. When you see him again, tell him I'm sorry, would you?"

"Yes, Daddy."

"I don't know what came over me. It's just . . . well, you know the two of you aren't supposed to be in here alone together."

"I know, Daddy."

"I like Cole. He's a good kid. But, sweetheart, you have to understand . . . the mind of a teenage boy . . . well, just trust me on this."

"I know, Daddy," Stacie said again.

"If you know, why was he here?"

"He'd walked me home from the library," Stacie began, reciting the story she had rehearsed in preparation for this very conversation, "and it was hot outside, and he wanted some water. I let him in to give him some, and . . ."

"Okay, stop," Stacie's father said. "I guess I don't need all the details. Just . . . I need you to promise me that this won't happen again."

"It won't, Daddy. I promise."

"You're all I have left. I can't lose you, too. Do you know what I mean?"

Stacie nodded her head, instinctively glancing at the

two empty chairs around the kitchen table. A lot had changed in five years.

Stacie had gotten up in the middle of the night to use the bathroom. As she opened her bedroom door, she could hear her mother and father talking. Even at eleven, she could tell from the tone of their voices that it was something serious.

She quickly turned around in the dark room and woke her thirteen-year-old sister, Mya.

"Wake up!" she whispered loudly.

"What?"

"Just get up!"

The two girls got up and stood near their slightly ajar bedroom door, listening to their parents.

"I thought I should come to you first, Clark," Stacie heard her mother say, "before you go finding out from some stranger."

"How long have you been seeing him?" Clark responded, an apprehensive tone in his voice.

There was no answer.

"How long?" He raised his voice.

"A year."

The girls heard a crash. Stacie moved to go into the hallway and see what was happening, but her big sister held her back.

"I love him, Clark, and, like I said, I . . . I think we

should get a divorce," Stacie heard her mother say.

"Don't you even think you're taking my girls. Just because you want out doesn't mean they're going with you," Clark said, raising his voice even more.

"No, I understand. You've always been a good father. They should stay here with you."

There was silence for a long time. Stacie glanced questioningly at her older sister.

"Just wait," Mya whispered.

They heard keys jingling.

"It doesn't make sense for me to continue sleeping here. I'll get my things together over the next week."

"What about the girls?" Clark said.

"I'll talk with them."

Stacie and Mya heard the front door open.

"You'll be getting the divorce papers within the next two weeks. Let's not drag this out any longer than we have to, okay, Clark?"

He did not answer.

"I'm sorry," Stacie heard her mother say weakly, and then the front door closed.

The girls looked at each other, confused. They stood in their bedroom doorway listening, the door now all the way open. Silence. Then, on bare feet, they took slow, cautious steps across the hallway. Still they heard nothing until they reached the entrance to the living room, where they saw their father slumped on the living room sofa, his back to them. Stacie quickly ran to him, Mya right behind her. They stopped just in front of a shattered lamp. The big, blue lamp that had once rested on the table next to the couch now lay in three large, sharp pieces, its shade smashed in on one side. The girls looked at their father and saw tears streaming down his face.

Stacie and Mya quickly stepped over the broken glass and sat on either side of him, wanting to console him, but not knowing how.

"I'm sorry, babies," he said, pulling them close to him, crying even harder. "I'm so sorry I let her leave you."

"I want to ask you a question," Clark's voice brought Stacie's mind back to the present. He had gotten up from the breakfast table and was now standing right next to her.

"Yes?"

Clark scratched his head and shifted nervously. "Are you . . . are you . . . having—"

"No, Daddy." Stacie shook her head. "I'm not."

Clark seemed relieved. "Is he asking you to do . . . that? Is he trying to pressure you?"

"No, Daddy."

"And even if he did, you'd tell him no, right?"

"I would tell him no."

"Good. Just remember what happened to your sister," Clark said, grabbing Stacie's book bag off the back of the chair and holding it out to her.

Stacie took the bag, shouldered it, and walked slowly toward the front door.

"One more thing," Clark said. "Tell Cole that I'm sorry I grabbed him like that, but you also tell him that if he tries to pressure you in any way to do anything that you shouldn't be doing, he will get a lot more than a firm shake and a talking to."

Chapter Two

COLE STEVENS stood at the open door of the refrigerator, holding his bowl of Lucky Charms in one hand and using the other to pour milk over the sugary cereal. His mind was still on what had happened with Stacie's dad the day before.

He put the milk back in the fridge, closed the door, and turned around to find a shirtless man standing inches from him. He was nearly twice the size of Cole's sixteen-year-old frame, even though they were almost the same height. The man's chest was wide and chiseled, his stomach tight, his arms thick, a fat vein running down the length of each bicep.

"Good morning, Cole," the man said. He stretched the neck of a white T-shirt over his head, then pulled it down over his torso.

"Edric." Cole didn't say anything else, just carried his bowl over to the table, took a seat, and started eating.

"Do you mind if I have a bowl?" Edric asked, with exaggerated politeness.

"Do what you want."

Edric took a bowl out of the cabinet, found a spoon, and pulled the milk out of the fridge. He prepared himself a small amount of cereal and sat down across from Cole.

"Look, I'm trying here, Cole," Edric said.

Cole continued spooning the cereal into his mouth, doing his best to focus all his attention on the cartoon on the back of the cereal box.

Edric moved the box aside so he could look directly at Cole.

"I said, I'm trying. I don't know what more I can do. I've been seeing your mother for almost a year."

"Eight months."

"What?"

"You said almost a year," Cole said, looking Edric in the eye for the first time. "You've only been dating her eight months."

"Okay. You got me. I've only been seeing her for eight months. I thought that would've been enough time for you to get to know me, long enough for you to have grown to like me."

Cole just stared blankly into Edric's face.

"Is there something that I've done to offend you?"

"Yeah."

"And that is . . . ?"

"How about it's the first thing in the morning, and you walk half naked out of my mother's bedroom. You don't live here, and you ain't married to her."

"Maybe one day that'll change."

"Well it ain't changed now."

Edric looked as though he were thinking over what Cole had said. "Would you like for me never to spend the night again?"

"Yeah. I'd like that a lot," Cole said, with a little more attitude than he had intended.

Edric stood and extended an open hand to Cole. "I'll talk to your mother about that, see how she feels."

Cole thought about just leaving him hanging, but he decided to shake the man's hand, even though he didn't want to.

"I hope that will help to make things a little better between us."

"Maybe," Cole said.

Edric grabbed his bowl of uneaten cereal from the table and dumped its contents down the garbage disposal. Then he grabbed his jacket off the back of one of the kitchen chairs and walked out the front door, without saying another word to Cole.

The moment Cole heard the door close, he was out of his chair and heading quickly down the hallway toward his mother's room.

He didn't knock, just pushed the door open.

His mother was startled out of her sleep. She was wearing a nightgown, but when she saw Cole standing at the foot of her bed, she quickly yanked the blankets up to her chin.

"Cole, what are you doing in here?"

"That man just walked out of this house!" Cole said angrily, pointing a finger toward the kitchen. "You said he wouldn't be spending the night here."

"Cole," his mother said, sitting up in bed and lowering the blankets some, "it was late. We were tired. It didn't make sense for Edric to drive home."

"But you said—"

"I know what I said, Cole, but things change."

Cole shook his head in frustration. "Ma, he's no good for you. I don't like him."

"All he's tried to do is become your friend. He's a really nice man. You'd know that if you'd just give him a chance."

"I don't like the way he comes around here and acts like he owns the place. He don't pay no bills up in here. He tries to act like he's my father. I got a father."

"Cole," his mother said, swinging her legs over the side of the bed, "you have to understand—"

"No. I don't like the way he treats you. I don't like the way you let him treat you!" Cole said, his voice cracking. "You walk around in short skirts, serve him dinner, bring him drinks. You weren't doing all that for Pops before he left."

"Why do you keep bringing him up? He's been gone more than three years. No one has heard from him. He's probably dead, for all we know."

"He's not dead," Cole said.

"How do you know? He hasn't called, or tried to contact us. How do you know?"

"Because I just do, and you shouldn't disrespect him by having some man sleeping all up in your bed."

"Disrespect him?" Cole's mother looked as though her son had said something completely offensive. "Disrespect him?" she repeated, now getting to her feet. "Do you know the harm that man did to us, and the even greater harm he could've done if I didn't get rid of him when I did?"

"I know," Cole said, turning away from his mother. "You told me a thousand times, and, frankly, I'm tired of hearing you criticize my father."

"Cole, turn around."

Cole didn't respond, just stood staring intently at a spot on the wall.

"I said, turn around," his mother said, a little more forcefully.

Cole slowly did as he was told. His mother took hold of him gently by the shoulder.

"I don't mean to criticize your father. I just feel you should know the truth, and I can't help it that it happens to be hard to hear. I wish things had turned out different. Truth is, I never stopped loving your father." She touched her son's face. "He was my first true love."

"Then why are you with this other man?"

"Because life goes on, Cole. I'm lonely. . . . I need companionship. Edric and I have fun together. And I'm going to keep seeing him. I'm going to see him again tonight, as a matter of fact."

"And what about Pops?"

Cole's mother pulled her hand from his face and shook her head. "He's gone, Cole. I've accepted that. I think it's time you did the same."

Chapter Three

"COME UPSTAIRS. I want to show you something."

Stacie hurried to keep up with her best friend, Donesha, who was bounding up the stairs in excitement.

After the way the discussion about Cole had gone down with her father, Stacie had had too much on her mind to go home and do homework. She had to talk it out, so she'd gone to the one person she knew would have something to say about it.

Donesha led Stacie into her bedroom, where, on the full-size bed in the middle of the pink room, a bunch of Macy's shopping bags were laid out.

"Went shopping, girl!" Donesha said, posing by the bed as if getting ready for someone to snap a picture of her. Then she quickly started pulling items one by one out of the bags, with Stacie still standing in the doorway.

Stacie and Donesha had been friends for almost three years, ever since halfway through freshman year, when they'd realized they had a common acquaintance.

Donesha and Cole had gone to the same grammar school. They'd actually used to date, but Donesha always insisted it was never a big deal. "We barely even kissed; we were so young." For Stacie, it was just good to have someone to talk to about boys and other stuff.

"Come on over here," Donesha said, frantically waving a hand of freshly painted pink fingernails toward Stacie.

Donesha was attractive in her own faux-Hollywood sort of way. She would get her brown-blond-streaked hair done in a different style every week. While at the salon, she'd get a manicure and pedicure and have her eyebrows waxed.

She wore only designer clothes, and M•A•C makeup.

Donesha was in her element, pulling boxes out of shopping bags, the dozen or so metal bangles on her wrists making more noise than tin cans tied to the back of a newlywed couple's car.

"Dang, how much money did you spend?" Stacie asked,

coming over to the bed to have a closer look at her friend's latest acquisitions.

"I don't know. Five, six hundred. You know I use my father's debit card. His form of child support."

Donesha opened a Coach box and pulled out a brown cloth-and-leather purse. She looped it over her shoulder. "You like it, girl?"

"That's just like the one my father bought for my birthday," Stacie said, not sure the similarity was entirely a coincidence. Stacie loved her best friend, but Donesha sometimes had an annoying habit of appropriating other people's wish lists.

"I know! When I saw it, I was, like, why should Stacie be the only one with that fly Coach?" Donesha reached back into the bag and pulled out a pair of black pumps. They just happened to be the same pair that she and Stacie had seen at the mall the other day. The pair that Stacie had said she was going to save her money for. "What you think?" she said, holding the pair up.

"They're great," Stacie said, not as enthused as she tried to sound.

"I know you said you were going to get them, but I didn't know how long it would take you to save the money, so I was, like, I could just get them now, and you could borrow them whenever you want."

"Really."

"Yeah, girl. I was looking out for you."

"I appreciate that," Stacie said.

Donesha began clearing the bags from the bed and went over to her walk-in closet to find room for her purchases. From inside the closet, she said, "So, what's going on with you, anyway? How's Cole? I thought you guys were supposed to be planning for the big day."

"There might be a problem," Stacie said, sitting awkwardly on the edge of the still cluttered bed.

"What did you say?" Donesha said, quickly turning around in the closet doorway.

"I said, there might be a problem."

Donesha ran over to Stacie and hugged her tight. "Good! I've been telling you, you shouldn't rush into anything, and I'm glad you listened."

"I didn't listen to you. It's just . . . my father caught us in the living room yesterday. . . . After the way he reacted, I just don't know what he'd do if he were to find out we actually had sex."

"So, don't have sex. What's the problem? Is Cole pushing you to do it? Boys, that's all they want with their no-good butts."

"No, it's not like he's pushing me or anything. Like I said—"

"Whatever the reason," Donesha said, cutting Stacie off, "I'm glad you changed your mind." She sat beside her on the bed. "You're sixteen. What's the rush? If Cole doesn't understand, then fire his ass. You got the rest of your life to have sex. Take your time."

"You didn't," Stacie said. "You started having sex at fifteen."

Donesha smiled, ignoring the veiled insult in her friend's remark. "I don't have a hang-up about sex like you do. I enjoy it."

Chapter Four

AFTER SCHOOL on Tuesday, Cole stood outside the double doors to the cellar of his friend Marc's house. This was where Marc usually brought girls when he wanted to have some "alone time" with them. And now Cole stood nervously by the door, almost afraid to go in.

He thought about the trip to school that morning. As was his usual practice-day routine, he'd walked to school with three of his friends and teammates from the football team. They liked to gather for a hearty breakfast at a nearby diner before class, in preparation for what were sometimes very grueling practice sessions. They walked slowly, back-packs slung across their shoulders, their baggy jeans sagging from their hips, each of them wearing extra-extra-large football jerseys.

"Dude, you serious? Stacie's old man walked in on y'all when you was about to get some?" Tony, six feet tall with his hair in cornrows, said.

"Snuck up on us real quiet. Like a damned ninja in stealth mode. I had her shirt up, was about to get that bra off, and then her Pops was, like, standing right in front of us. But I was cool, though," Cole said, trying to downplay the incident and move on to another topic.

"You wasn't scared?" Drew said, shooting Cole a look of exaggerated disbelief. "I bet Stacie's old man grabbed you and put you in a headlock. And you was, like, 'Please, please, mister, don't hurt me.'" Drew wrapped his own hand around his throat to demonstrate his point.

"It wasn't nothing like that. I got up off the sofa, straightened my gear, and me and her Pops stepped outside, and had a little man-to-man. He said he don't want me there when he ain't around, and I told him I think I could handle that," Cole explained, trying to stay as close as possible to what actually happened.

"Man, I don't get it with you," Marc said. He was the first-string wide receiver on the team, tall, thin, and muscular. He was the one Cole connected with the most, both on the field and off. "Why you go through all that trouble trying to get it from that girl, when you know her old man would kill you if he caught y'all?"

"Because he loves her," Drew yelled, jumping up behind his three friends. "Cole's in love!"

"Whatever, man," Cole shot back.

"It's cool, man. Ain't nothing wrong with that," Marc continued. "But does she love you?"

"Of course she does," Cole said. "What do you think?"

"I think she don't," Tony said, stepping in front of Cole.

"What do you know?"

"Last time I heard, you ain't hit it," Tony said, elbowing Cole in the gut.

"That ain't none of your business."

"Considering everything you goin' through, that ain't a bad question," Marc said. "You hit that yet?"

"Naw, not yet," Cole said.

"Dude, you crazy," Drew said. "All the women that be sweatin' us just because we on the football team? I gotta be turning down women, and you know I hate to do that. You *know* I hate to do that!" He shook his head, a look of wistful sadness on his face.

"Well, I ain't interested in them other girls," Cole said. There were definitely other girls. He was often surprised at how bold freshman and sophomore girls could be, going as far as slipping notes and pictures into his locker. *Please meet me after school,* some of the letters would say, along with accompanying snapshots of girls in supertight jeans and tiny T-shirts. Cole would take those letters and simply throw them in the nearest trash can, unless they were signed. If he could read the signature, he would find the sender and give her back her note or picture, letting her know that he already had a girlfriend and that he wasn't going to cheat on her.

In truth, he did love Stacie. Besides, cheating was wrong. Cole's father had taught him that before he was even able to understand what his father meant by it.

"Cole, don't worry about it, man," Tony said, throwing an arm around Cole's shoulder. "There was a time when all the rest of us were virgins and scared to have sex. Ain't nothing wrong with waiting till you're married." He cracked a smile and looked at Drew, and they both burst out laughing.

Cole smacked his friend's arm off his shoulder.

"I ain't scared to have sex, all right? In fact, after today, I probably ain't gonna be no virgin no more."

"Today's the day?" Marc asked.

"We've been talking about it. I asked Stacie to meet me at your spot after practice, since we can't hang out at her place anymore. Is that cool?"

"Cool. I ain't got nobody coming over. Did you tell her where the key is?"

"Under the big rock, to the left of the door."

"Right," Marc said.

"So you gonna hit it?" Tony said.

"What you think?"

"Yeah, right. I'll believe it when you have some proof," Drew said.

"Aight, then . . . maybe I'll give you this when I'm done with it." Cole reached into his deep jeans pocket, fished around a bit, and pulled out a condom as his friends whooped and hollered.

Now, standing outside of Marc's basement door, Cole was holding that same condom in his hand.

He took a deep breath, exhaled, and slid the little packet back into his pocket. Pulling open the wooden door, he stepped carefully down the cement steps into the dark basement.

When he got down, it took a while for his eyes to adjust to the blue light emanating from the lone bulb in the room. He knew Stacie must have come down there already, because the latch was off the door.

"Stacie?" Cole called.

"I'm right here," came her reply. He looked to his right and saw her in one of the darkened corners, sitting on an old wooden chair. Even in the darkness, he could see something that resembled sadness on her face. He walked over to her, gave her a hug, and kissed her on the lips.

"How you doin', baby?"

"Fine," Stacie said, receiving the kiss and hugging him back.

"Why don't you come sit with me over here on this mattress?" Cole asked, taking her hand and leading her across the room. They sat down on the edge of the mattress, and Cole kissed her on the side of the neck. "Was your father really mad the other day?"

"He was mad, but he didn't do anything. All we did was talk."

"He told me I better not be over at your house again if he's not there," Cole said, "but I think everything will be cool." Cole paused for a moment, wondering how he should proceed next. He started kissing the center of Stacie's neck, and slowly baby-kissing her lower and lower, unbuttoning her shirt.

When he got to the third button, Stacie grabbed his hand and moved it away.

"We shouldn't do this right now."

"Why not?" Cole said, sounding a little more frustrated than he'd meant to. "We keep talking about it."

"I know, but why can't we just wait?"

"What are we waiting for? You know I love you. Why can't we just do it?" Cole said, trying to kiss her on the neck again.

"Because," Stacie said, pulling herself up from the mattress. "We can't." She turned away from him and rebuttoned her shirt.

"Is this because of what happened the other day?" Cole asked, getting up from the mattress. "Any dad would have reacted like yours did. You're his little girl."

"No!" Stacie said, raising her voice as she turned to face Cole. "It's because my father said that if you try to pressure me into doing this, he's going to do more than talk to you next time. And I believe him."

Cole was quiet for a moment as Stacie's words sank in. "I'm pressuring you? I thought you wanted this . . . just like I did."

"I do. But my father said—"

"I heard what your father said, Stacie. So what? That means you gonna break up with me?"

"No, of course not. I just don't think it's the right time for us to be taking such a big step."

"Okay, fine," Cole said. He was disappointed, but he really did want to try to see things from Stacie's perspective. He lowered himself back onto the mattress, leaned back against the wall, and opened his arms. "Then just stay with me awhile, and we can hold each other."

Stacie looked down at him, his hands reaching for her. She looked conflicted as if she were considering each of his words carefully.

"No, Cole, we shouldn't. I should really be going." She grabbed her book bag and headed toward the basement door.

"Stacie," Cole said, getting up to stop her.

"Don't, Cole," she said, opening the door. "Just leave it alone for now. I'll see you at school tomorrow. We can talk about it then or something. . . . I love you." For some reason, Cole thought her words lacked a ring of sincerity.

Cole closed the door and threw himself back onto the mattress. His mind was swirling with questions. Was he really trying to pressure Stacie into doing something she didn't want to do? Didn't she feel safe around him? Why didn't any of his friends have this kind of problem with girls? Wasn't he as much a man as they were? And how could Stacie say she loved him if she didn't even want to be around him?

Chapter Five

I HOPE DAD isn't in a bad mood, Stacie thought, as she stood at the front door of her house, preparing to walk in. After leaving Cole earlier, she hadn't been quite ready to go home, so she'd stopped off to see how her sister, Mya, was doing and to check out her little niece, Tiffany.

It had been a year since their father had kicked Mya out of the house.

Stacie remembered standing outside their father's door, holding her sister's hand, just as Mya was about to tell him the news.

"Can you come in with me?" Mya asked, squeezing Stacie's hand.

"Sure, I can," Stacie said, though she felt more scared than she let on.

Mya walked into the room without knocking, pulling Stacie behind her. Their father was in bed, wearing a T-shirt, business slacks, and dress socks, and reading *Time* magazine.

Stacie could tell that he knew something was wrong. She saw the suspicion in his eyes.

Mya did not allow their father to speak first. She confessed what she had to, turning her face to the floor as the words tumbled out of her. When she was done, she stood there, silent, apprehensive, her hand squeezing Stacie's, waiting for their father to explode.

Strangely enough, he didn't. He sat watching the two girls for what seemed like a full five minutes before he spoke, but when he did, his voice was calm, almost soothing, as if he'd been planning his speech all day.

"First of all, did you really think you had to expose your little sister to this?"

"I wanted her to be in here," Mya said.

"Fine. This is not a problem. In the morning, we'll call Doctor Bill, and we'll have this taken care of."

"I'm not having an abortion, Daddy," Mya said, her voice respectful, but firm, her eyes still locked downward.

It seemed to Stacie that her father didn't even hear Mya. He just continued calmly making plans for the next day. Mya interrupted him and repeated that she was not going through with it. He said she was. She said she wasn't. He yelled. She screamed. There were tears, and horrible things were said. Stacie remembered their father saying something about their mother, how she had left him. Mya tried to tell him that that was a different situation, but their father said the circumstances were close enough. He said he couldn't deal with coming home every day and watching his daughter throw her life away. Mya would have to either abort the baby or leave. Mya left.

After leaving Cole, Stacie found herself standing in the hallway of the run-down apartment building in which her sister lived. When Mya opened the door, Stacie walked in, her head lowered, looking downright melancholy. She dropped herself down on the living room sofa.

"He wants to have sex," Stacie finally said, shaking her head.

"Who, your boyfriend?" Mya said, closing the door. "You didn't do it, did you?"

"No. I said, he *wants* me to, not that I did it already."

"Well, do *you* want to?"

"Does it hurt?"

Mya chuckled, then said, "Um, well . . . that's beside the point. Do you love him?"

"Of course I do. But I'm scared, too."

"That's natural," Mya said, placing her hand over Stacie's, trying to soothe her. "But if he loves you, I think he can wait."

"That's kinda how I've been feeling," Stacie said.

They were quiet for a moment. Stacie glanced at her sister out of the corner of her eye, guessing what her next question would be.

"How's Daddy? He ask about me?" Mya said.

"No," Stacie hated to admit. But she wasn't going to lie to her big sister. "You should go over there, talk to him."

"Uh-uh. He doesn't want to see me, or my daughter. We don't want to see him, either."

"How is Tiff?"

"She's fine. She's in there, sleeping," Mya said, walking into the kitchenette and grabbing a tissue. She dabbed her eyes. "You can go in. Just try not to wake her."

Stacie tiptoed into the bedroom. Mya's full-size bed was pushed against one corner, Tiffany's crib against the other.

Stacie stood over the wooden crib and looked down at her niece, who was wearing nothing but a diaper, her hair pulled into two pigtails wrapped in pink ribbons.

She placed her palm on the infant's warm back and felt her breathing. Tiff was beautiful, and Stacie loved her, but she didn't know how her sister did it—raised a child all by herself. If nothing else, it gave Stacie just one more reason not to rush into having sex with Cole.

Stacie unlocked and pushed open the front door of her house. It was late, almost nine o'clock; her father would be a little upset that she had not called him. It didn't matter, though.

Spending time with Mya always made Stacie a little mad at him for the way he'd treated her sister.

Stacie walked into the living room and was surprised not to see her father there, watching MSNBC as he normally did at that time of night.

She walked into the kitchen, then tried his den, softly calling out to him, but he was nowhere to be found.

Maybe he's upstairs in his bedroom, Stacie thought, wondering at the same time why he would be in bed that early.

Reaching the top of the stairs, Stacie halted; she thought she heard some shuffling noises—not from her father's room, which was to the right and down the hall, but from her bedroom.

Stacie walked slowly toward her bedroom, hearing what now sounded like thrashing noises getting louder and louder. She heard someone muttering under his breath and realized that her father was in her room. But what was he doing there?

Stacie stopped in front of her bedroom door, which was slightly ajar, and with trembling fingertips pushed it open.

She could not believe what she saw. Her room looked as if a tornado had hit it.

Everything that had been hanging neatly in the closet was now strewn across the bedroom floor. The bed itself was a mess. Every drawer was hanging out empty from the dresser, and in the middle of it all stood her father.

When he saw Stacie, he froze.

Her eyes opened wide, her mouth gaping, Stacie slowly walked to the middle of the room. She turned in a slow circle, surveying the damage around her.

"It's not what you think, sweetie," Clark said hesitantly. "I was just looking for—"

"For what?" Stacie asked, her eyes now angrily focusing on her father. "For what, Daddy? For something you can use to throw me out of your house, too? What were you looking for? You think I got a baby in here?"

"No, sweetheart," Clark said, stepping toward his daughter, his arms extended.

Stacie stepped back from him. "You come home, find me and Cole kissing, and now you're going through my stuff like you can't even trust me anymore."

"I do trust you, Stacie."

"Do you? Then what's this?" Stacie almost screamed.

"When your mother left—"

"I don't want to hear about my mother!" Stacie cried, almost hysterical. "Why are you doing this to *me*?"

"I'm doing this because you're all I have left. I love you so much, and I'm just trying my best not to have you walk away from me like . . . like the others."

"You just don't understand, Daddy. They didn't leave. You drove them away, and if you keep on doing what you're doing, you might do the same to me," Stacie said, wiping tears from her face. She turned and ran out of the room.

"Stacie!" Clark called, running after her.

She had already made it to the front door by the time he got to the top of the stairway.

"Where are you going?" he said.

"Out. I can't stay here tonight."

"Don't you walk out that door, young lady, or else—" her father said.

"Or else what? You won't ever let me back in? Do what you have to do, Daddy," Stacie said; then she slammed the door behind her.

Chapter Six

THE NEXT day after practice, Cole, Drew, Tony, and Marc were in the locker room getting showered and dressed.

"You see that pass Cole threw to me?" Marc said, tossing a pair of rolled up socks in the air and cradling them as they fell into his arms. "How long of a touchdown pass was that?" he asked Cole.

"Seventy-eight yards," Cole said, not quite as excited as his friend.

"But did you see that rundown tackle I almost had on you?" Drew said, swatting the roll of socks out of his hand.

"The key word is *almost*," Marc said, snatching the socks from the floor. He sat down on the bench to put on his shoes.

"Yo, you guys up for heading over to The Plaza after this? The new Jordans just came out. I might wanna pick up a pair."

"Y'all go ahead," Cole said, leaning over on the bench to tie his shoelaces.

"C'mon," Tony said, twirling a bath towel in his hands, then snapping the tip of it at Cole. "You need to get that Stacie outta your head. Get back in the game. There might be some nice females up there. Somebody that'll give it up to you before you turn sixty." Marc and Drew hooted at this last comment, and Tony playfully snapped the towel at Cole again.

This time, however, Cole grabbed it, yanking it out of Tony's hand. He stood up and gave his friend a serious look. "I said, I ain't going. And you need to be keeping Stacie's name out your mouth."

"Or what?" Tony said, walking up to him, getting in his face.

Drew quickly ran over and placed himself between his friends. "Whoa, whoa, whoa! C'mon, y'all, chill. We boys up in here, right?"

Cole and Tony both kept their eyes on each other and acted as though they hadn't heard what Drew had said.

"I said, we all boys in here, right?"

"Yeah," Cole finally said under his breath.

"Yeah," Tony quietly rejoined.

Drew slapped both Cole's and Tony's shoulders and said, "Aight, hug it out, if y'all cool."

Cole and Tony shook hands, then gave each other a quick hug and a slap on the back.

Marc stepped over, tossed his keys at Drew, and said, "Why don't y'all head out to my truck? I'm gonna holler at Cole for a second."

Drew and Tony walked out, leaving Marc and Cole in the locker room.

"Have a seat, man," Marc said, lowering himself beside Cole on the bench. "You talk to her at all today?"

"Just for a second at lunch," Cole said. "I told her I had to see her. That we need to talk. So she's meeting me at my house after this."

"You gonna try to hit it again?"

"I mean, I don't want to keep asking her, like I'm begging or something."

"Naw," Marc said, "I ain't saying do that. This is your *girlfriend*. She say she loves you, she should be wanting to give you some, show you that, prove that to you."

"Yeah, I know. You right," Cole said.

"But what if she still don't want to?"

"I don't know."

"It's your business to know. Dude, you gonna be seventeen in a minute, and you still walking around without your first piece. That ain't right. Everybody know y'all kickin' it, and everybody know you ain't hittin' it. You know how that's making you look?"

Cole shook his head. "I never thought about that."

"All the girls in this school puttin' out, and you toying with Stacie." Marc rested his hand on Cole's shoulder. "Don't get me wrong, Stacie is cool people, one of the coolest females up in here, but you got to man up and let her know what the deal is, bro."

Cole turned to look at Marc. "What do you mean?"

"I mean, later, when y'all at the house, if you decide you want some, you ask her for it. And if she decides she's still playing games, and don't want to give it to you, you let her know what's up. You tell her you love her, but you ain't no child no more. You a man with needs, and if she can't satisfy them, then you'll have to find somebody that will. You feel me?"

It took Cole a moment to answer, but he finally said, "Yeah. I feel you."

"Good," Marc said, squeezing his shoulder. He stood up.

Cole stood as well.

Marc gave his friend a slap on the back, grabbed his gym bag from his locker, and turned to leave the locker room. "And let me know how that works out."

"Sure thing," Cole said, adding under his breath, "if it works out."

Not an hour later, Cole lay on his bed with Stacie on top of him, both of them fully clothed. They had managed to make small talk for about five minutes before their hormones got the better of them. They'd been making out for twenty minutes, and Cole was beginning to want to feel more than the fabric of Stacie's clothes.

He reached up, brought her close, passionately kissed her lips. She did not pull away until he started to unbutton her shirt, trying to reach around to undo the clasp of her bra.

Stacie quickly leaned up, putting a halt to everything. "What are you doing?"

"Relax, baby. Just getting you a little more comfortable."

"For what?"

"Come on, what do you think?" Cole said, starting to get a bit frustrated.

Stacie climbed off him and walked barefoot across the room. She folded her arms over her chest and turned to face him. "Why would you do that when you know where it could lead?"

"Because . . . what's so wrong about it leading there?" Cole asked; he had gotten up, too, and was standing just in front of his bed, not even trying to hide the bulge in the front of his jeans. "Every time we get together and we kiss and grind on each other, this happens," Cole said, pointing down at his pants, "and nothing else. I always end up with an agonizing case of blue balls and have to take a cold shower."

"I'm sorry," was all Stacie had to offer.

"We're almost seventeen years old. Baby, we've been together almost three years," Cole said, walking over to her and gently taking her by the shoulders. "I love you."

"I love you, too."

"Then why can't we show it? Why can't we prove it?"

"Why do you need proof that I love you? My word isn't good enough?" Stacie pulled away from his touch, as though she were offended by what he'd just said.

"I'm not saying that. But I want to feel you. I want us to experience that special connection for the first time together." Cole took a few steps back. "Why don't you want that with me?"

"You heard what my father said."

"Every father says that. When I'm a father, I'm gonna say that. But if every father had his way, there would be no more human race, because their daughters would not be having sex, and no babies would be made."

"Exactly, Cole. Babies. What if I get pregnant?"

"Stacie," Cole said, practically begging, his hands on her shoulders again, "I'll use protection. We'll be smart. We'll be safe. Whatever you want me to do, I'll do it, so you won't have to worry about a thing."

Stacie looked down at the floor, as if giving it some serious thought.

"I love you, baby. Just say yes, and everything will be fine."

Stacie looked up at him. "Cole . . ." she began.

"Yes, baby," Cole said, kissing her quickly on the cheek. "Anything."

"I can't."

Cole froze. Whatever hope he had been feeling a moment earlier was now quickly seeping out of him. He thought about what his boy Marc had said. He wondered if he really wasn't being man enough about his business.

Cole dropped his hands from Stacie's shoulders and took a step back.

Stacie must have sensed his shift in attitude. "Cole?"

Cole swallowed hard. He wasn't quite sure what he wanted to say, but he felt he had to say something. "Baby, I've told you I love you, and I'm not going anywhere. But you keep pushing away from me. I'm almost seventeen years old, and yes, I do have physical needs. You're the girl that I want to fulfill those needs with, but you keep telling me you can't. I love you, baby . . . and I just don't want to have to find someone else who won't keep pushing me away."

Chapter Seven

WHEN STACIE walked up to her house and saw her father's car in the driveway, she thought about turning around and just walking in the other direction, but she figured they had to run into each other eventually.

After their big blowup, she had spent the previous night at Mya's. She'd called to let him know where she was, but only out of respect, and she'd told him as much.

He had told her to come home, so that they could talk things out, but Stacie didn't want to talk. She told him she just wanted to spend some time with her sister and her niece.

Now back, Stacie closed the door behind her, put her book bag down, and walked quietly into the house, not calling out to let her father know she was there.

Walking into the kitchen, she saw her father at the table, hunched over an old framed photo of himself and Stacie's mother. It was their wedding portrait.

Stacie walked around the table to stand next to him, but he did not acknowledge her, just kept holding the frame gently in both hands, looking down at it as if transfixed by the memory of that day.

"Dad? You okay?" Stacie asked.

"You said I drove her away. Do you really believe that?"

"I was saying that to hurt you, Daddy. I don't think that."

"No. You were right," Clark said, still gazing down at the portrait. "I loved her too much. I smothered her. She was always talking about her independence, saying that she needed some form of life outside of mine. But I wouldn't let her have it. I thought she'd go out there and find somebody else. And funny . . ." He chuckled pathetically at himself, bringing a hand to his eyes to wipe away a tear. "That's exactly what she did."

Now Stacie was beginning to tear up, too. For some reason, she felt as if her dad's words held some special meaning for her.

"Will you forgive me for going through your things like that?"

Stacie hesitated before answering. "Daddy, those were my personal things."

"I know. It was wrong. But forgive me this time. I promise I'll trust you more. I promise." Clark stood with his arms open.

Stacie allowed herself to be hugged.

"When you left, I thought I had driven you away, too," her father said, kissing her on the side of the face.

"No, Daddy. I'm not going anywhere."

That evening, Stacie went to bed very early; she was worn out from everything that had happened during the day.

She was glad that she had come to some form of reconciliation with her father. He told her he had gone through her things because he was trying to figure out where she had been so late in the evening. Initially, he'd been looking for Donesha's number, to see if Stacie were over there. But then his imagination had run away with him, and he'd had flashbacks of finding her in a compromising situation with Cole the other afternoon.

Clark admitted to Stacie that his search for a phone number had changed into a search for condoms or birth-control pills.

"I'm not having sex, Daddy," Stacie insisted. "I already told you that."

"I know that, but I could not help myself. I'm sorry."

But as Stacie lay in bed staring up at the ceiling, she felt a tear creep out the corner of her eye and slide down her face.

On the one hand, she was glad that she could tell her father that she was not having sex and know that it was true. But the same question kept popping up in her head. Who was she really abstaining for? Her father? Or herself?

Stacie had been devastated after Cole said what he'd said earlier that afternoon. At first, she couldn't believe what she was hearing. Had he really insinuated that he would sleep with someone else if she wasn't willing?

"Can we sit down and talk about this? Please, Cole?" Stacie had begged, practically in tears.

Cole was already getting her shoes for her. "Baby, I just don't know what more there is to say. I've told you how I feel. It's up to you to decide now."

Stacie sat up in bed now, in the dark, and wiped her tear-streaked face with both hands. She might end up losing Cole, and for what? Because she was afraid to make love to the boy she said she loved? How ridiculous was that?

Her father told her that she shouldn't be having sex. But Cole was right. Every father told his daughter that.

Stacie tried to think it through. If they used protection, there would be no threat of her getting pregnant like Mya. So there really wouldn't be any harm done.

But if that were the case, why was she still scared? Why was she still having second thoughts?

It doesn't matter, she said to herself. You love him, that's what counts.

Filled with new resolve, she settled back onto her pillow and started making plans in her head. Tomorrow would be the day. Tomorrow she would tell Cole that she was finally ready to give him what he needed.

Chapter Eight

COLE WAS driving his '94 Accord like a man pos-
sessed. He wanted to get to Stacie's house as quickly as
possible.

After they'd parted on such a sour note the previous
afternoon, he'd been really conflicted. He needed to talk to
her, set everything straight, find out where her head was.
Deep down, he had to admit, he was also curious to know if
she'd given any more thought to what he'd said.

But when he got to her house, he saw her father's old
blue Mercedes parked in the driveway, and he lost his resolve
to go through with it. He sped past the house, hoping her
old man wasn't peering out the window at that moment.

He stopped once he got to the corner. He grabbed his cell phone from the passenger seat, flipped it open, and started to call her. But he knew he was taking a huge risk. Stacie's father didn't allow her to have a cell phone, and Cole didn't want to get her in any more trouble by calling her late at night. He turned the car around and headed back home.

As he pulled up to his house, however, Cole became even more irritated. Edric's Cadillac was parked out front.

Cole exited his car and slammed the door harder than he normally did, cursing the fact that the man didn't seem to have a house of his own. Cole let himself in to the house, intending to go straight to his room to avoid seeing Edric or having to say anything to him.

As he closed the front door behind him and took a step into the living room, however, he saw Edric sitting on the sofa with his legs draped across his mother's. She seemed to be wiping tears from her eyes.

"Ma, you okay?" Cole asked, moving quickly across the room, ready to do whatever he had to if he learned that Edric had done anything to hurt her.

His mother again dabbed the corner of her eyes with the tissue she was holding. She looked up at Cole and smiled. "Everything's fine, baby. Something wonderful just happened."

Cole looked across at Edric, who had a big grin on his face.

"Should I tell him, or do you want to?" Cole's mother asked.

"No, you do the honors, Lana," Edric said, squeezing her hand in his.

"Cole, why don't you have a seat?"

"Ma, would you just tell me what's going on?"

"Okay, okay. Are you ready? Edric just asked me to marry him! And I said yes!"

Cole felt as though he had just been punched in the gut. He literally couldn't breathe for a second. He felt a little wobbly on his legs. Glancing down, he saw the tiny ring box on the coffee table, the shiny diamond on his mother's finger.

"What?" Cole said.

"Your mother said that we're—"

"I didn't ask you," Cole said, pointing a finger at Edric. "I asked my mother."

"Cole, please don't speak to Edric that way."

"Ma, we didn't talk about this. You didn't tell me that you had any plans of marrying this man."

"I know, Cole," Lana said, unable to wipe the smile from her face. "He surprised me. It came from nowhere, but—"

"If you marry him, where is he going to live?"

"We haven't discussed the details yet, but I think Edric will move in here," Lana replied, turning to Edric for confirmation. He nodded his head.

"No! This is Pop's house. He bought it. What about

him?" Cole said, almost yelling. "He moves in here, I'm moving out. It's him or me, Ma!"

"Cole, don't do this," Lana said, getting up from the couch, the smile now gone from her face.

"No, Ma. You gotta make a decision," Cole said, staring at Edric with hate-filled eyes. "Either he goes, or I do."

"Cole, I said, don't do this."

Cole looked at his mother for a long moment, feeling tears threatening to come to his eyes. But before that happened, he turned, stormed off to his room, and slammed the door.

An hour later, Cole was lying in bed, his pillow folded around his head, when he heard a faint knock at his door.

He didn't bother to respond, knowing full well it was his mother.

After another, louder knock, he heard her voice from the other side of the door. "I'm coming in, like it or not. I hope you're decent."

Cole heard his mother enter the room. He turned and looked up at her, standing near the foot of the bed.

"Cole, I'm sorry, but—"

"You told me when you first started dating him it was nothing serious."

"It became serious."

"But why do you have to rush into marrying him? Do you love him?"

Lana sighed. "It's not as simple as that, Cole."

"Then explain it to me."

"It's complicated."

"That's not good enough," Cole said.

Lana sat down in the chair beside her son's bed. "You have to understand, Cole. It's been getting harder and harder to manage this household on just one salary ever since your father left—"

"Pops didn't leave. You kicked him out," Cole interjected.

"This second income will help us a whole lot, Cole."

"And what about Pops?"

"Cole, you keep bringing him up, but we haven't seen or heard from him in three years. Obviously, he's moved on."

Suddenly, Cole sat up, kicked his legs over the side of the bed, and faced his mother. His tone became much more serious. "Mom, can I ask you a question?"

"What's that?"

"You say you haven't seen Pops in three years, right? That you don't know where he is?"

"What are you getting at, son?" Lana said.

"How can you marry Edric if you're still married to Pops?"

"We, uh, got a divorce."

"But you kicked him out," Cole reasoned aloud. "One day he's here, the next he's gone. In order to get a divorce, doesn't he have to sign paperwork and stuff?"

Lana froze a moment, then began to stammer and stumble before finally getting out the words, "Because we could not find him, the law said I didn't need his signature."

Cole stood up, walked across the room, and looked out his window. "Mom, I can't stop you from marrying Edric, but if you know where Pops is, could you just tell me?" He turned to look back at his mother. "Please?"

Lana looked sorrowfully at her son, held out her hand, and said, "Cole, come here. Sit down."

Cole did as he was told.

Lana took Cole's hands in hers and said, "The only reason I've been keeping this from you is because your father did not want you to know. He was ashamed. But I'm going to go ahead and tell you anyway. I think you're old enough by now. I last saw your father six months ago." She sighed. "At the homeless shelter downtown."

"Can you call Stacie? I need to talk to her right now."

Cole had his cell phone pressed against his face, his grip tight and feverish.

Donesha was on the other end of the line. Cole had called her trying to get in touch with Stacie. It was the only way he could think of reaching her.

"Cole, what's wrong? You sound upset. Did something happen?

"Can you just call Stacie? It's a long story."

"I have the time, if you want to tell me, Cole."

Cole took a minute to tell Donesha everything that had just happened. About his mother agreeing to marry Edric, and about her hiding from him the fact that she knew where his father had been all this time.

"I'm so sorry, Cole. I remember your father from when he'd drop me and you off at the movie theater. I can't believe he's homeless."

"Neither can I," Cole said, grateful to hear compassionate words from someone. "Now, can you call Stacie? I have to go down there and try to find him."

"Tonight? It's late, Cole. The place—"

"I don't care!" Cole said firmly. "I have to at least try."

Donesha was quiet for a second on the other end; then she spoke up. "Okay. I understand. I'll give her a ring, then call you right back."

"Thanks, Donesha. I appreciate it."

Not three minutes later, Cole's cell phone was ringing.

"What did she say?"

"I didn't speak to her. Her father said she was in bed and not taking any more phone calls tonight."

"Damn," Cole said. "I don't want to go out there by myself."

"I can go," Donesha offered.

Cole thought about it for a second. "You sure?"

"Of course! How long have we been friends?"

"Since sixth grade."

"That's right. Ain't nothing I won't do for you. So come on and pick me up. I'll be waiting."

The homeless shelter was not much more than a vast single room that looked like a warehouse or airplane hangar. It was lined with rows of dozens and dozens of cots, occupied by men of all ages. Some of them were dressed in heavy coats, despite the unseasonably warm weather, sitting around and making small talk. Others were stripped down to sweatpants and undershirts and were tucked under their blankets, ready to retire for the night.

Cole and Donesha walked slowly up and down the aisles, looking at each of the men, hoping to find Cole's father.

Not having any luck, they went to inquire at the night director's desk. Cole addressed the wrinkled, heavyset man on duty. "Is there a Franklin Stevens staying here tonight?"

The man grabbed a clipboard from his desktop and thumbed through the few legal-sized pages before saying, "No. I don't see that name."

"Do you know if he's been here over the past six months? My mother said this was the last place she saw him."

"I don't know, kid," the man said, looking a bit put out. "We have records, but they're locked up right now. You can come in tomorrow, or call, but it's about to be lights out in fifteen minutes, so I doubt you're gonna find him tonight."

Cole lowered his head and had turned to leave when Donesha said, "Well, can we continue to look around for him till then?"

The man leaned back in his chair, then glanced down at his watch, as if contemplating.

"Please," Donesha said, "my friend hasn't seen his father in three years. We'll be out by ten o'clock. I promise."

"All right, go ahead. But at ten, lights are out."

Cole asked half a dozen of the homeless men if they knew a Franklin Stevens, and all of them either shook their heads or said they'd never heard of him.

At two minutes to ten, Donesha tugged at Cole's shirt and nodded toward the front door. The night manager was standing in the doorway, pointing at his watch.

Cole was standing near a gangly, bearded man, who was sitting on his cot, folding dirty clothes and putting them neatly in a plastic grocery bag. Cole gave the man a description of his father, but still, no luck. "Naw, never heard of a Franklin Stevens."

"Thanks, anyway," Cole said, disappointed.

"Hold on a sec," the man called out, stopping Cole and Donesha before they could leave. "I do know a guy fitting that description named Stevie Franklin."

* * *

The Accord was parked outside of Donesha's house. Cole and Donesha were inside with the windows rolled down, the moonroof pushed back.

Cole leaned back in the driver's seat staring up at the stars, not certain if he should feel depressed that his father was homeless or elated that at least he was one step closer to finding him.

Cole felt a touch on his hand and glanced over to see Donesha looking at him.

"The man said he stays there every now and then."

"But who's to say that he's even my father?"

"Just like you said, he probably switched his name because he's embarrassed. He fit the description exactly. Don't worry about it, you'll find him."

"Thanks, I appreciate that," Cole said.

Donesha leaned over and wrapped her arms around him. "Don't worry about it."

Cole hugged her back, then pulled away. "Stacie should've been here with me tonight. She tell you what's been going on with us lately?"

"No," Donesha said. "But I'll talk to her tomorrow. You need to be going home, so I can get inside." She got out of the car, then leaned in through the passenger window. "I'm sure if Stacie could've been here, she would've wanted to be," she said, smiling. Then she turned and walked up the path to her house.

Cole waited till she had gotten inside before driving away.

I hope she's right, he said to himself as he approached the corner. I hope she's right.

Chapter Nine

As SOON AS third period got out, Stacie waited in the hall by Donesha's locker, fighting against the wall-to-wall mass of students pushing up and down the corridor toward their next classes.

"Hey, what's going on, girl?" Donesha said, reaching around Stacie to spin the combination on her lock.

"I had a talk with Cole yesterday evening." Stacie spoke softly, leaning against the neighboring locker.

"Really. What about?"

"Well, he basically told me that if I didn't want to have sex with him, he was sure he could find someone else who would."

Donesha had been rifling through her locker, but she stopped when Stacie said this. She turned to face her friend. "He said that?"

"Yes."

"Those exact words?"

"Pretty much."

"What do you think he meant?" Donesha asked.

"Exactly what it sounds like."

"So what are you going to do?"

"I don't want to lose him, Donnie." Stacie sighed. "But if that was the only reason I decided to sleep with him, then that would be wrong."

"Right. I totally agree."

"But I thought about this all night. I do love him. And if I love him, isn't it okay?" Stacie smiled. "I mean, isn't it natural for two people in love to want to express their love in every way, including physically?"

Donesha didn't respond immediately; she just stared at Stacie as though she were speaking another language.

"Donesha?"

"I don't think you should do it. Two days ago, you said you didn't want to do it. What about your father? What if you end up pregnant like your sister, and your father kicks you out? This is stuff you really need to think about."

"Well, I changed my mind. Plus, my father won't find out. It's not like I'm going to tell him. And we'll be safe, so I won't get pregnant."

The school bell rang, announcing the beginning of the next class period.

"I've thought this through, Donnie. I'm telling Cole the good news at lunch."

"I still wouldn't—" Donesha tried to object again, but Stacie cut her off with a quick, giddy hug.

"Don't want to be late for science. See you later, girl."

An hour later, at lunch, Stacie finally caught up with Cole in his favorite corner of the school cafeteria.

As soon as he saw her, he told her he had big news, but she told him she had something important to say, and she insisted on going first. She couldn't wait to see his reaction when she told him.

He had a skeptical look on his face, as if he were expecting Stacie to tell him that she had thought about it and she still wasn't ready to lose her virginity.

Stacie smiled, unable to contain herself.

"What's so funny?" Cole said.

"I know exactly what you're thinking. You are so easy to read."

"I ain't here to play games with you, Stacie," Cole said, a little impatient.

"'I ain't here to play games with you, Stacie,'" Stacie repeated, deepening her voice in a playful attempt to imitate Cole. "Oh, stop being so serious." She gently punched him in the chest. "I just wanted to tell you that I'm ready to do it."

"Do what?" Cole said, seeming clueless.

"You know," Stacie said, blushing. "*It*. Do . . . it."

Suddenly Cole's face brightened, and his eyes opened wide. "You mean, *it*? That's what you mean? Make love?"

"Yes, Cole," Stacie said, so happy to see Cole's reaction that she couldn't tell which one of them was more joyous.

Cole hugged her around the waist, hoisted her up, spun her around three times, and kissed her on the mouth.

"I love you, baby," Cole said.

"I love you, too." She was so excited that she didn't even remember to ask him what it was that he wanted to tell her.

Chapter Ten

AFTER SCHOOL, Cole dropped Stacie off at her corner (they were nervous about how her dad would react to his taking her directly home), then drove to his place, where he found his mother in the kitchen, stirring something in a small pot at the stove.

It smelled delicious. Cole's stomach growled, but he controlled himself. He took a seat at the table and waited for his mother to speak to him.

"Are you going out to look for your father again?" Lana finally asked, not turning away from her cooking.

"Yeah."

"I really wish you wouldn't. He knows where you

are, and when he's ready to see you, he told me that he'd contact us."

"Why would you do that to me?" Cole asked, turning in his chair to face his mother. "You knew how much I missed him. Why would you keep him from me?"

Lana stepped away from the stove, wiped her hands on a towel, and sat down beside her son. "I know you're going to have a hard time forgiving me for that, Cole. But your father begged me not to tell you. Like I said, he was terribly ashamed of how things had turned out, and he couldn't bear the thought of you ever finding out." She laid her hand over Cole's and squeezed. "I did it because that's what he wanted, not to hurt you. You know I'd never want to hurt you."

She leaned over, kissed Cole on the cheek, then got up and stepped over to a cabinet. She pulled out some plates. "Having baked chicken tonight. Why don't you go and wash up?"

"Naw, if you don't mind, I want to go by the shelter again, see if Dad is over there."

"I'd really prefer you didn't go . . . but I know I'm not going to talk you out of anything regarding your father. I'll leave a plate for you in the oven."

Cole started out of the kitchen, but then stopped. "Ma, why don't you come with me?"

"I can't, Cole," Lana said, her voice heavy with sadness. "It almost killed me to see him the way he was six months ago. I don't know if I could take that again. Besides, I would feel a little guilty, considering I'm going to be marrying Edric soon."

"You don't love Pops anymore?"

Lana stepped across the room to stand next to Cole; she looked him straight in the eyes and said, "I've never stopped loving him and don't think I ever will. He gave me you. But things are different now. He's moved on, and now it's time I do the same."

"With Edric?"

"Yes," his mother nodded.

"I don't like him, Ma."

"And I'm sorry about that, but he's going to be your stepfather soon, so you're going to have to get used to it." She gave him a faint smile.

Cole tried his best to smile back.

"You sure you don't want to stay for dinner? Edric is on his way, and he'd really love to spend some more time with you."

"Naw, Ma. I'm fine."

When Cole left the house it was dark outside. He knew he had to do something about this marriage situation soon. Ever since his father had left, Cole had always harbored the hope that his parents would one day reconcile. But if his mother actually went ahead and married Edric, Cole knew there would be practically no way his mother and father would get back together.

He spent the entire ride over to the shelter trying to think of ways he could get his mom to give his dad another chance. His mind was still blank when he pulled up to the curb and parked.

When Cole approached the night manager's desk, the heavyset man recognized him. "How can I help you tonight, young man?"

"I was here last night, looking for my father, Franklin Stevens. I just wanted to know—"

"Oh, yeah," the night manager said, exerting a good deal of energy to stand up from his chair. "Just a minute. I got someone who wants to see you."

"Is it my father?" Cole said, excited.

The manager smiled and said, "Just wait here a minute."

Cole started to feel anxious. Was he really going to see his father again, after all this time?

One of the most vivid memories Cole had of his father was from a few years earlier, when his father had lost his job. Franklin Stevens had never gone to college, but he was skilled as a construction worker. He was not, however, a member of a union, and during one particularly rough patch of not being able to find work, he was forced to stand on the corner day after day with other workers for hire during the hard Chicago winter, all of them hoping to find jobs.

After a couple of months of working an average of only one day a week and spending as much on lunch and transportation as he made on his check, he became frustrated.

Cole's mother kept telling his dad that things would work out, that he should try to keep his spirits up. But Cole remembered his father pulling him aside and telling him how much being out of work was hurting him.

"I'm from a family that believes the man should be the head of the house," he said one night while Cole's mother was out late working a second job. "A man can't be a man if he doesn't bring in any money." He looked deep into Cole's eyes, then placed a hand on his shoulder before turning and heading for the front door. Cole heard his father mutter, as he was walking away, "What sense does it make me being around if I can't contribute?"

"What did you say, Pops?" Cole asked, wondering what his dad meant by his little speech.

"Nothing, son. Just go to bed," his father replied, without turning around.

Not long after that, instead of coming straight home from work, Cole's father began spending what little money he earned on drinks at a bar. He would often come home drunk, yelling and cursing the fact that he couldn't find steady work and that life was unfair to him.

Many nights, Cole would hear his parents arguing from his bedroom.

"All you do now is come in here drunk," Cole heard his mother say one evening. "You don't do nothing. You don't help around here. All you do is drink and pass out on the couch."

"If that's all I do, then maybe you can do things around here better by yourself," Cole's father hollered back.

"Maybe I can."

Cole had to squeeze his pillow around his head to force himself not to listen any more that night.

The next morning, Cole woke up to find his mother cooking breakfast as she always did, but he didn't see his father sitting at the table; he didn't even see a place setting for him.

"Ma, where's Pops?" Cole asked.

His mother continued cooking at the stove as though she hadn't heard what he had said.

"Ma? I said, where's Pops?"

She turned around this time, gave him an oddly vacant look, then turned the stove off and moved the skillet aside.

"Come with me, Cole," she said, walking past him and into the living room.

Cole followed his mother, thinking that she was going to take him to his father, but instead she said, "Sit down."

Cole sat on the couch.

His mother went to the hallway, pulled something out of the center drawer of a desk, and came back to sit down beside her son.

"Do you know what this is, Cole?" his mother asked, opening her hand to expose a hypodermic needle, a tiny white rock in a plastic vial, and a bent spoon, the curved bottom of it burned.

Cole shook his head.

"It's drugs. Your father was acting strange lately. I knew he had been drinking, but it seemed like it was more than that. I looked through his things, and this is what I found," his mother said, scooting over a little closer to her son. "That's why he's not here. I put him out."

"You did what?" Cole cried.

"Cole, he wasn't helping this family anymore, and I was able to deal with that. But the moment he stopped trying, the moment he gave up on himself and started taking this drug, was the day he actually started hurting us. I told him to go, and to not come back as long as he was using."

Tears spilled from Cole's eyes.

His mother wrapped her arms around him. "I know you don't understand now, but I pray one day you will, son. I pray one day you will."

"Cole?"

The familiar voice pulled Cole out of his thoughts and back into the present.

When he glanced up, Cole was looking into the face of his father, who was standing in front of him, a slight smile on his face.

Cole immediately threw his arms around the man, hugging him tightly.

Franklin hugged Cole back, squeezing him hard. He

clapped him on the back three times. "All right, all right," he said, slowly easing away.

Taking a step back from his father, Cole got a good look at him. He expected to see a man like many of the other men in the shelter, skinny from malnourishment, dirty, and unshaven, with unkempt hair. But Franklin did not look like that at all. Yes, he was thinner than Cole remembered him, and his hair was a little matted, but his clothes were clean, and he looked in relatively good health.

"How you been, Pops?" Cole said, not having a clue as to what else to say.

Franklin looked at the night manager and said, "It was good seeing you again, Mr. Macklin." To Cole, Franklin said, "Come with me."

Cole followed his father through the door.

"How did you get here?" Franklin asked.

"My car," Cole said, pointing down the street to the corner.

"Let's go there."

Franklin did not say a word, just walked beside his son till they reached the old Accord.

"Patrick, the man you spoke to last night, told me you were looking for me," Franklin finally said. "Why?"

"What do you mean, why?" Cole said.

"Your mother wasn't supposed to tell you where I was. I told her I'd contact you guys when I was ready to see you."

"What? I thought you'd be happy to see me," Cole said,

not sure how he himself was feeling anymore. "One morning I wake up, and you're gone. Ma showed me the drugs you were taking. In three years you don't even give me a phone call, write me a damned letter. I come down here looking for you, and you ask me why?"

"Calm down, son," Franklin said, reaching out to Cole.

Cole swatted his arm away. "Don't tell me to calm down."

"I said, calm down," Franklin said, grabbing Cole a bit more forcefully this time.

Cole took a deep breath and listened.

"Look, I'm sorry I disappeared like that," Franklin said. "I'm sorry I let things get away from me. Sorry I had to force your mother to put me out. But she was right. The first two and a half years I was gone were hard for me. I was homeless, addicted; I didn't care if I lived or died. But six months ago, your mother found me. She had divorce papers with her. I signed them, but doing so made me realize I wasn't ready to give up on the life I had. So I got in a program, started helping out at this hardware store down the street, doing small chores for them. I don't live at the shelter anymore, but I got my own room at a halfway house." He smiled proudly. "I'm even taking a course down at the community college, thinking about getting my degree."

"That's good, Pops," Cole said. "But that don't explain why you never called."

Franklin lowered his head in shame. "I was about to. In,

like, a month. I would've finished my first semester of class, would've been clean for six months. I was going to surprise you and your mother. I was going to wear some nice clothes, bring roses, tell her why she should take me back. And we were going to be a family again. But don't you worry, I'm still planning on doing that. Just don't tell your mother."

Cole looked up at his father; despite everything that had happened, he felt sorry for him. "You ever think about why she came to you asking for a divorce?"

"No. I just figured she didn't want to be married any-more."

"No, Pops. She didn't want to be married to *you* any-more. She's been seeing this new guy. They're planning on getting married."

Chapter Eleven

THE NEXT day, two hours before Cole was supposed to pick her up, Stacie sat in Donesha's living room making final preparations.

"So I told my father you and me are going to the movies, okay?

"And you're sure you really want to go through with this? In a hotel, of all places? That seems kinda hoochie, don't it?"

"Cole's friend's brother works at reception and got him a huge discount on a really nice room. I think it's going to be romantic."

"And what if your old man calls my cell phone?"

"Just don't pick it up," Stacie said. "We're supposed to be in the movies. Knowing that, he probably won't call."

Stacie looked out Donesha's window for Cole's car. When she turned back, she found her friend staring at her.

"What?"

"You don't feel guilty about lying to your father?" Donesha asked.

Stacie thought about the question. She had figured she'd be okay with it, but she couldn't help feeling a little guilty. After the talk and reconciliation she'd had with her father, it was understood that they would be honest with each other. Stacie was going back on that promise.

"I do feel a little guilty," Stacie admitted to her friend. "But I'm trying not to think about it too much. I'm sure the feeling will pass, and I'll be fine."

"But what if he finds out?" Donesha persisted. "He'll be pretty disappointed in you, won't he?"

"He won't find out."

"You sure?"

"Yeah, I'm sure," Stacie said.

Just then, Stacie heard a car horn honking outside. She leaned across the sofa, parted the curtain, and looked out. "That's Cole. I gotta go."

An hour later, Stacie stood behind the door of the hotel bathroom, wearing a lingerie set she had excitedly bought from

Victoria's Secret just for this occasion. She had showered with a peach-mango bath gel; she applied a strawberry-scented baby oil while she was still wet, and then, after drying off, spritzed herself lightly with her favorite perfume.

Cole knocked on the door twice to ask what was taking her so long.

She called back, "Don't rush perfection. I'll be out in a second."

A moment later, she stepped into the room, her heart pounding so loudly she wondered if Cole could hear it.

The room was dark, but with the aid of three candles that Cole had set up, she was able to see her way to the bed, where Cole was sitting, naked from the waist up.

He threw his legs over the side of the bed and stood up to meet her.

She walked slowly toward him until they were barely an inch away from each other.

They stood at the foot of the bed looking into each other's eyes, their lips partly opened, breathing heavily, their hearts racing.

Even though Stacie was certain it was warm in the room, her body was freezing, gooseflesh covering the parts of her that were exposed—practically her entire body.

She had no idea what to say or do next, so she waited for Cole's lead.

He finally spoke. "You okay?"

"Yes," she said softly, not entirely sure.

Cole moved even closer to her, lowered his face, and kissed her.

It was an awkward kiss for Stacie, but not because of anything Cole had done. It was as if Stacie had forgotten what to do, as if her lips wouldn't move, as if she had no feeling in them.

Cole didn't seem to notice. Stacie felt his hands around her waist now, gently urging her down on the bed.

She let him move her, allowed her legs to follow his instruction.

She ended up on her back, staring up at the dark ceiling, watching the faint, fuzzy circles of light created by the dancing flames of the candles.

She concentrated on those patches of light as she felt Cole's body weight on top of her. She felt his warm tongue on her neck, kissing her, sucking her, harder and harder. She almost raised her hand to push him away, but he stopped on his own, probably thinking about what her father would do if he left a mark.

Cole kissed her lips, her chin, the front of her neck; then she felt his kisses on her chest. He kissed every part that was left exposed by the bra, running his tongue along the sloping line of it.

A moment later, the bra popped open, and her breasts fell out. She heard Cole gasp, felt him press his jean-clad hips against her bare leg.

He baby-kissed his way down the center of her stomach, kissing the crest of each of her hips.

He grabbed the sides of her panties. Stacie raised her hips and he slid the panties down her legs, tossing them onto the floor.

He continued to kiss her on the belly and the hips, and then he parted her legs.

Stacie's eyes opened wide, wondering what he was going to do. She didn't know what to do, what to feel, what to say.

Cole raised himself up from between her legs, moved off the bed, and slid his jeans and underwear off.

He placed his body back on top of Stacie's, kissed her on the cheek once, then pushed himself up so he could look down into her face.

"You ready?" he asked, his voice barely above a whisper.

Stacie didn't even try to answer, just nodded her head slightly.

He pushed himself all the way up, so that he was kneeling in between her parted knees.

Stacie was cold, her body shivering now; something told her that this wasn't how it was supposed to be.

She tried to ignore her apprehension as she had been doing all night, but the thought of her father had managed to get into her head again. She saw him standing behind her, staring at her as she walked out to the car at Donesha's house, giving her that look that seemed to say that he knew exactly what would be going on tonight.

Stacie heard the sound of something tearing; she looked up and saw the condom packet being ripped open between Cole's teeth.

He loves me, Stacie told herself. He said so. This will be okay.

Cole was back on top of her, heavier this time, excited. He brushed against her leg, and she felt the cold lubricant of the condom smear her thigh.

I told him that I was ready, Stacie thought. But what would happen if I were to stop him now, if I were to just tell him that maybe we should wait—

He was shimmying in between her legs now, trying to make room for himself. She felt him pushing open her thighs with his warm palms.

Stacie turned her head to the side, shut her eyes tight.

Don't think about it, she told herself. Just don't think about it, and it'll be over in a minute, and then I'll be a woman, and I'll be able to keep my boyfriend.

She continued to tell herself that, over and over and over again, until she felt the cold, latex-covered tip touch her where she had never been touched by anyone else before.

Stacie's eyes shot open. She couldn't believe what she saw. It was her father, standing in the room, witnessing this entire event.

"No!" Stacie shouted all of a sudden, barely recognizing her own voice.

"What?" she heard Cole say. She didn't answer him,

didn't even acknowledge him, just pushed up, squirmed, and slithered till she was out from under him. She backed up into a corner of the bed, her knees pulled toward her chest, her arms wrapped around them.

"What's wrong?" Cole said, startled.

"I can't do it," Stacie said. "I can't."

Chapter Twelve

DONESHA SAT in her bedroom at her mirror, just staring at herself.

"You're pretty," she said to her reflection. "You're beautiful, and you're smart, and you're sexy."

Donesha spoke these words of affirmation out loud, but a voice in her head kept casting doubt. If she were so sexy, it asked, then why was Cole making love to Stacie right now, instead of her?

One by one, Donesha started to pull off the dozen metal bangles she wore on her wrists, repeating to herself, "He loves me? He loves me not? He loves me?"

Cole had been her boyfriend from sixth grade through eighth grade.

At the time, he'd said he liked her a lot. But Donesha had always loved him. Truly loved him.

The summer after middle-school graduation, Cole told Donesha that he didn't think they had that much in common anymore, and they broke up. She cried as though she had just been told that someone she loved had died.

She had felt as though a part of herself had died. She just couldn't accept it. She approached Cole while he was playing basketball at the park one day. Pulling him aside, she told him she would give him anything if they could just be boyfriend and girlfriend again. She would even have sex with him, do whatever he wanted her to do. But Cole didn't go for it.

She went as far as telling Cole that she didn't want to keep on living if they weren't together.

"I hope you don't mean that," Cole had said, though he still didn't agree to get back together with her.

But even at thirteen, Donesha wasn't one to make idle threats.

"He loves me? He loves me not?" Donesha continued counting the bangles as she stared at her reflection in the mirror.

Slipping the final bracelet over her hand, she announced, "He loves me!"

She raised her forearms up to shoulder level, her wrists facing the mirror, where she could see the now-healed scars.

Donesha's mother had found her unconscious on the bed, her wrists haloed by two circles of blood that soaked deep into the white mattress.

The ER doctors were able to stitch the wounds in time and save her.

The rest of that summer for Donesha was spent away, in therapy.

While in therapy, she'd harbored plans of winning Cole's heart again once school started. When she heard that Cole had gotten together with someone else, however, she found herself thinking that all hope for her was lost. Little did she know she would end up befriending the very girl Cole had chosen to be with.

Still looking at herself in the mirror, Donesha wondered what Stacie and Cole were doing at that very moment. Had they already started? Were they doing it? Had they finished? Were they in bed cuddling?

Donesha looked over at her cell phone.

Stacie had lied to her father. That wasn't right. Especially after her father had specifically told her not to have sex with Cole.

Donesha picked up the phone and flipped it open. She wondered how Stacie's father would have reacted if he had had any clue as to what his daughter was doing right then. She smiled to herself as she thought of how clueless he was about his own daughter's life.

She punched in Stacie's home number. She looked at the

number on her screen for several long moments, wondering what she would say if Stacie's father picked up.

She caressed the SEND button a few times with her thumb, coming very close to pressing it. "Hmm . . . should I?"

Finally, she said, "I won't. Not this time."

Chapter Thirteen

THE NEXT DAY at lunch, Marc sat with Cole on one of the benches outside.

Cole was miserable. He had no idea what had happened with Stacie the previous night. She'd never given him a full explanation for the way she had reacted.

He'd driven her home, or at least to the corner of her block, and she'd just kept repeating, "I'm so sorry, but I couldn't," the entire way.

Now Cole was getting ready to go and talk with her, and Marc was trying to give him what he thought was the best advice for the situation.

"Didn't you tell her that there are other girls who would go with you in a heartbeat?"

"Yeah, but—"

"And did you mean it?"

"Yeah."

"So, how do you think she'll view you, if you just let this ride and continue to wait for her?" Marc said. "She gonna look at you like you was a punk, and you'll never get any. You gotta let her go."

"But I don't want to let her go," Cole said, sad and confused. "That's not what I want, and I don't think it's what she wants."

"Okay, fine. Then you keep her on. Don't change the fact that you're a man, and you need what you need. And you gonna get it, whether you like it or not. Your body is gonna demand it. So you end up sleeping with some other girl, maybe two or three different girls. You don't tell Stacie about it, because you still love her, and you don't want to hurt her. But Stacie finds out. My old man told me that women always find out if you cheating. So she gets hurt, and you get hurt for her hurting. Only difference is, this way you were being dishonest, instead of being up front and letting her go now."

It was unfortunate, but everything Marc was saying made sense to Cole.

Marc nudged Cole's elbow. "Here comes your girl," he muttered under his breath.

Cole looked up and saw Stacie walking across the lawn toward them.

"Hey, Stacie," Marc said politely as she approached. He stood up and said, "I'll catch y'all later," then left. When he was out of Stacie's line of vision, Marc looked back at Cole and mouthed the words *Handle your business*.

Stacie sat next to Cole on the bench. She looked around for a moment, as if she were just thinking about the weather, then finally said, "I know what he was telling you."

"No, you don't," Cole said, still conflicted about what to do or say.

"He was saying that since you told me you'd see other women if I didn't have sex with you, and I didn't, then you have to keep your word. Was it something like that?"

"Nothing like that," Cole lied.

"But that's where we've come to, isn't it? You're getting pressure from your friends. Girls coming up to you, offering it to you. And I'm stopping you from getting it, because you're trying to be faithful to me. Do you want me to . . ." Stacie wiped a tear from her eye. "Do you want me to break up with you, so you can have sex?"

"No, Stacie. I love you."

"But you want to have sex?"

"With you. Damn! With *you*, Stacie, why can't you get that? Why can't we just do that?"

Stacie sniffed, wiped at her eyes some more. "Because . . . we just can't."

"Fine. Then we don't have to. It's been this long, what's another however long? It's cool."

Cole didn't know what was wrong with Stacie. He had just told her everything was fine, but still, the tears did not stop.

"No, it's not cool, Cole. You need what you need. And whether you meant it the other day or not, just like you said, you're gonna get it from somebody else. I don't want to be around for that. So maybe it's best if we just—"

"If we just what?" Cole said, leaning in closer toward Stacie. "You're the one that doesn't want to have sex. Don't tell me that you're trying to walk away from me."

"I'm sorry, Cole," Stacie said, the tears coming even harder now. "I can't see you anymore." She got up from the bench and, with her hands covering her face, hurried away before Cole could stop her.

Chapter Fourteen

"**I**'M TELLING YOU," Donesha said, "don't call him!"

Stacie was in bed, a box of tissues between her knees, on the phone with her best friend. She had been crying; her entire face was red and tender. "But he said he didn't want to break up with me, and I ended it anyway."

"You did exactly what you were supposed to do," Donesha insisted. "Girl, you'd be the joke of the entire school. Yeah, you'd still be the girlfriend of the star quarterback, but he'd be sleeping with every girl on the cheerleading squad, and they'd be smiling up in your face just to stay next to him. I'm telling you, you did exactly what you were supposed to do. Trust me on this."

"Then why don't I feel that way?"

"Just like doing the wrong thing can sometimes feel good," Donesha said, "doing the right thing can sometimes feel bad."

Stacie lay back in the bed, Donesha's words doing nothing to comfort her. She knew she was being selfish. Judging by the look of surprise on Cole's face, he hadn't had any idea she was going to do what she did, and she couldn't erase the memory of the look of hurt on his face that still lingered in her mind.

"Can you do me a favor, Donesha?" Stacie asked, wiping tears from the mouthpiece of the phone.

"Anything."

"I was thinking, can you call Cole tonight, and tell him how sorry I am for having to break up with him? Or do you think I should take the chance and do it myself?"

"No. You don't want to go against your father's rules. Besides, you broke up with Cole. You calling him the same night, talking about you're sorry, will make you seem like a joke. Don't worry." Donesha smiled. "I'll take care of it for you."

Chapter Fifteen

LATER THAT EVENING, Cole sat with his mother at the dinner table, glumly picking at some baked pork chops and mixed vegetables. Cole hadn't spoken since they had said grace, and now his mother placed her knife and fork down on her plate and stared at her son.

Cole ignored her stare, lightly stabbing the chop with his fork.

"So, anything exciting happen at school today?"

"No," Cole said, without lifting his head from his food, choosing not to mention the conversation he'd had with Stacie.

"Is everything all right?"

"Everything's fine."

"So, have you had a chance to sit down and talk with Edric?"

Cole looked up at his mother. She was smiling, as if she imagined this talk to be like two guys walking down a tree-lined path toward the sunset.

"No, we haven't talked."

"He'd really like to get closer to you."

Cole didn't say anything, just lowered his head again.

"Do you think you'll ever like him?"

"Does it matter, Ma?"

"Of course it matters. He's going to be your stepfather soon."

"Who knows when that'll be? You said you didn't have a date set," Cole said, mostly under his breath.

"Cole, there's something I need to tell you. Edric and I were talking last night, and since we're just having a private wedding, with no planning, we decided, why wait? We're going to do it a little sooner."

"How much sooner?" Cole said, becoming worried.

"On the twenty-first of this month."

Cole did a quick calculation in his head, double-checked on his fingers, then announced with shock, "That's in two weeks!"

"Yes, that's right."

"But why are you in such a hurry to marry this man?"

"I've already been through this with you, Cole."

"But what if Pops came back?" Cole said. "You still love him, right?"

"Yes, I told you that. But I don't—"

"What if he came back and he wanted to try to work things out?"

"Cole, your father is a drug addict who's been gone for—"

"But what if he was clean, and wanted to start over?"

"But he's not."

"Can't you just play along? Just, what *if*?"

Cole's mother relented and closed her eyes for a second, as if imagining the possibility. A brief smile came to her face, and she said, "Okay, so I'd probably hear what he had to say."

"Are you serious?" Cole said, excited.

"Sure. He was my husband, after all. And deep down, I do love him. But I don't know why you're putting so much thought into this, because it's never going to happen."

Cole dug into his food, trying to hide the huge smile on his face, and said, "Just hopeful, I guess."

The bell over the door announced Cole's entrance into the hardware store where his father worked.

"Can I help you?" a man with dark brown skin, wearing glasses, asked from behind a tall counter.

"Is Mr. Stevens around?" Cole asked.

"He's out back, emptying the trash. You can go out that door if you like."

"Thank you," Cole said, following the man's directions.

At the shelter, after Cole had given his dad the news that his mother was planning to marry Edric, Franklin seemed to have lost all hope.

"It ain't over till it's over, Pops. Isn't that what you used to always tell me?" Cole had said, doing his best to console him.

Now, as Cole walked out into the alley behind the hardware store and saw his old man sweeping up, he found himself believing that maybe it really wasn't over, after all.

"Hey, Pops," Cole said.

Franklin, wearing blue work trousers and a matching button-down, short-sleeved shirt, turned around with a smile, surprised to see Cole. "What are you doing here?"

"Inviting you to dinner, the day after tomorrow."

"What? Where?"

"Home. I'll come and pick you up."

"Hold it. Is this your mother's idea?"

"No. She doesn't exactly know about it, but—"

"Then I'm not coming," Franklin said, waving his hands. "I thought you said she was about to get married."

"I know. But she doesn't really love that guy. She still loves you. She told me tonight. Even said that if you came back, and you were clean and wanting to work things out, she'd think about it."

"She said that?" Franklin said, unable to hide his obvious pleasure.

"Yeah, Pops. She did."

"But look at me. I'm not ready to see your mother again."

"Dad, you look fine. Get a shave and a haircut tomorrow. Buy a white shirt from Sears. You got enough money, right?" Cole said, about to dig in his pocket for his wallet.

"I'm fine with money, son, thank you," Franklin said. "But are you sure about this?"

Cole walked up to his father, clapping a hand on his shoulder and letting it rest there. "Dad, I could be as sure as I wanna be, but in order for this to work, *you* have to be sure. Are you, Pops?"

"Yeah," Franklin said, though his face betrayed his nerves. "I am."

The next day, Cole found it hard to concentrate at school. As soon as the last bell rang, he rushed out to his car and headed home.

He now sat in his car parked in front of the halfway house where his father lived.

After leaving school, he'd gone home to ask his mother if she had any plans that night.

When she told him she didn't, Cole had offered to fix dinner.

He'd prepared spaghetti, and when he was almost done,

he told her that he needed to go to the store to buy garlic bread.

"Just spread some margarine on some white bread, sprinkle it with garlic sauce, and stick it in the oven."

"That's ghetto, Ma," Cole had replied. He was using the store run as a ruse to get out of the house so he could pick up his father.

From his car, Cole continued to watch the front door of the halfway house.

When he saw his father emerge, Cole jumped out of the car and walked around to greet him.

Cole couldn't deny the fact that his father looked good. Almost better than he had remembered him. He wore a casual brown suit with a white shirt, the collar open. His black shoes were polished to a shine, and he had gotten a shave and a fresh haircut, as Cole had suggested.

Cole hugged his father tight, proud of all the effort he'd put in. "Pops, you look good, man. I mean, really good."

"Good enough for your mother?"

"Definitely. She's gonna be so surprised," Cole said, noticing something he hadn't a moment ago. "What's that, Pops?"

Franklin raised his left hand, looking at the ring on his finger. "Oh, that. My wedding band. After your mother had me sign those divorce papers, I took it off, but I guess I never considered myself divorced. I'm hoping it brings us some good luck tonight."

"Me, too, Pops."

* * *

Half an hour later, as Cole pulled up in front of the house, he noticed a strange look on his father's face as he stared out the window.

Cole cut the engine, waited a moment, then said, "Dad, you okay?"

"Yeah," his father replied, without turning away. "It's just that there were times when I never thought I'd see this place again."

"Come on, let's go."

"No, son, I'm serious. I had lost everything: my home, my wife, you. There were times when I seriously didn't know what else I had to live for."

"Come on, Pops, don't talk like that." Cole was shocked to hear such an honest confession from his father.

"That was then, son," Franklin said, reaching out, giving Cole's shoulder a firm squeeze. "I'm a new man now, and hopefully, after today, I can start to put things back where they need to be."

He jumped out of the car and slammed the car door confidently behind him.

Cole did the same.

"Son!" Franklin called.

"Yeah, Pops?"

"Let's go inside and have some dinner!"

With purposeful, confident strides, they both walked toward the house and up to the front door.

At the door, Cole was about to use his key, but decided instead to ring the doorbell. "Let's surprise her," he said to his father.

Franklin smiled and grabbed his son's hand, squeezing it for a moment, then said, "Thank you."

Cole could hardly believe that his family was on the verge of going back to the way things had been before. He felt incredibly happy.

He heard the door being unlocked from the other side. He held his breath, and he could sense his father doing the same next to him.

When the door finally opened, Cole's mother took one look at him and immediately asked, "Why are you ringing the doorbell when—" She stopped short as soon as she noticed the man standing beside her son.

Lana threw her hand over her mouth and stumbled backward in shock.

Her hand was trembling as she slowly lowered it to her side. "I thought I'd never see you again," she said softly.

"I guess you were wrong about that," Franklin said, smiling and opening his arms. "Now, how about a hug?"

There was no hesitation from Lana. She walked right into her ex-husband's arms. They held each other tight, rocking back and forth. Lana buried her head in Franklin's shoulder.

It's really happening, Cole thought, standing beside

them. He'd dreamed of this moment for so long, and now it was actually coming to pass.

Cole's parents finally disengaged from their hug, and now they just stared into each other's eyes, still holding hands.

"I'm sorry things had to happen the way they did," Cole's mother finally said, leading the way into the living room and closing the front door.

"Don't be sorry. You did what you had to do. I understand that."

"But I could've—"

"No," his father stopped her.

"I didn't have to—"

"Stop," Franklin said, bringing Lana's hands up to his lips, kissing her knuckles lightly.

Standing behind them, Cole pumped his fist in the air, fanatically mouthing the word *Yes!*

Everything was going according to plan.

Then Cole heard the lock on the front door turning.

He looked over his shoulder to see the door open, and cursed under his breath as he saw Edric walk into the house.

Edric came slowly into the living room, watching Lana, then Franklin, and then Cole, before stopping in front of all three of them.

"So, what's all this?" Edric asked, a plastic smile on his face.

"Edric, we didn't have plans to get together today," Lana said.

"Yeah, I know. But I missed you, and I wanted to see you, so I came by. I guess that was foolish of me, considering there was another man you were more interested in seeing."

"It's nothing like that, Edric. This is my husband. . . . I mean, ex-husband," Lana corrected herself. "Franklin."

Franklin held out his hand. "Pleasure to meet you."

Edric looked down at Franklin's hand in disgust. "Oh, *Franklin*. This the same Franklin you've told me so much about, Lana?"

"Edric, why don't you come back another—"

"No, no. I see we have a nice little family reunion going on, and considering that you and I are supposed to be getting married, won't that make me part of the family? Shouldn't I be here?"

"No problem, Edric," Franklin said. He turned to Cole. "Maybe this was a bad idea, son. I think I ought to be going. We can do this another time."

Franklin started to walk past Edric toward the door, but the larger Edric pressed a firm hand into his chest, holding him where he stood. "Please don't leave on my account. I was just about to reminisce about some of the stories I heard about you." Edric rubbed his chin. "Oh, yeah, I love the one about you being a heroin addict. Or how you lost your job three years ago, and at the first sign of hardship, you buckled and started hitting the bottle, then shooting up. Remember that, Franklin?"

"Pops, I'm sorry about this. Let's just go," Cole said, grabbing his father's hand and trying to pull him away.

"I said, ain't nobody going anywhere!" Edric yelled. He took a deep breath, then said, "Sorry to have raised my voice, but I just want Franklin to answer my question." He moved closer and stood toe to toe with Franklin. "Did you get hooked on drugs, forcing Lana to put you out on the street? And then, while you were gone, did you ever make even one attempt to come back, or to contact your son? Did you, Franklin? And I want you to answer me this time."

"Okay," Franklin said, his voice low and shaky. "You're right."

"Now, I know this may sound cruel," Edric said. "But it's actually for the sake of Lana and her son, because, by the looks of things, it appears that she might actually be toying with the notion of taking you back. She might have a fantasy that she could get back with you, and her son would have his father back, and everything would be perfect again. So what I'm doing is just reacquainting her with the way things really are, and how they always will be when it comes to you. You left. Never checked up on her or your son. Never sent money, not a single dime for child support, and now you're here as though you have a right to be. Do you get where I'm coming from, Franklin?"

Cole's father didn't say a word, just stared at the floor.

"I asked you a question, man. Answer me!"

"He don't have to say nothing," Cole said, stepping between his father and Edric.

"Get from in front of me, boy," Edric said, pushing Cole and sending him stumbling against the wall.

"How dare you? Get out of my house!" Lana said, startling Edric.

"What? But I was just talking to the man," Edric pleaded, quickly shifting gears and acting as though he and Franklin were merely chatting over a beer.

"Get out of my house, or I swear I'll never speak to you again."

Edric gave Lana a long, hard look. He turned and glanced at Franklin, then Cole, and said, "Fine, Lana. I'll leave. But you make sure and call me when this man leaves."

"Just . . . go." Lana walked over to the door and opened it. As soon as Edric walked out, she slammed the door behind him. "I'm sorry, Franklin."

"No. It's okay. I really need to be going, anyway. Cole, would you drive me back?" Franklin said, walking toward the door.

"Pops, just stay," Cole said. "I made dinner and everything."

"Yeah," Lana said. "You don't want all that food to go to waste."

"C'mon, Pops."

Franklin pulled the door open.

"Franklin," Lana said, "give us one reason you won't stay."

Franklin turned, a serious look on his face. "Because, like Edric said, I don't deserve to be here."

Cole sat with his father in a diner across the street from Franklin's halfway house. Franklin's plate sat untouched in front of him, while Cole picked at the occasional french fry in his hamburger-dinner platter.

"Pops, let's get out of here. You aren't even eating."

"No," Franklin said, as he had the last three times Cole asked. "We were supposed to have dinner tonight. I'm not going to have you missing a meal just because of me."

Cole sat quietly in front of his father, a half-eaten french fry in his hand.

After a moment, Franklin sighed heavily, then said, "Hell, maybe I deserved this." He raised his eyes to meet Cole's. "Maybe I needed this to open my eyes to what I've done."

"What are you talking about? He didn't have the right to say those things about you."

"He didn't? Why not? They were all true."

"Pops . . ."

"I'm a joke. I shouldn't be able to even call myself your father."

"C'mon, now."

"Like that man said, when was the last time I sent your mother child support?"

"You were homeless. You didn't have a job."

"I have one now. I haven't sent you guys anything," Franklin said, looking disgusted with himself.

"But you were about to start, weren't you?"

Franklin lowered his head again and said softly, "I don't know. I should've at least checked on you, come around every now and then. Me choosing to stay away is the only reason that man is in the house; it's the only reason your mother is about to marry him. It's all my fault." Franklin's shoulders sagged. "But maybe it's better this way."

"What did you say, Pops?"

"Nothing." Franklin stood up from his chair and pulled from his pocket the tattered old wallet he had from back when he had had a decent amount of money to carry around in it.

He slid six dollars from the billfold and put them on the table.

"Come on, son. I think it's time we both got home."

Chapter Sixteen

THE NEXT DAY, after the end of first period, Stacie grabbed her books off the desk and hurried out of the room. She made her way quickly down the hall, weaving among the hordes of students until she was able to see Cole's locker.

He was not there; she hoped she had not missed him.

The previous night she had not been able to sleep a wink. She had lain in bed thinking about everything that had happened between them: the three years they had known each other, the time they had spent falling in love. She had finally realized that she was not ready to give all that up just because they were having a little trouble trying to decide what they would do about sex.

At 4:40 a.m., she'd dragged herself down the hallway to use the bathroom. Afterward, she had stared at herself in the mirror. Her face was pink and puffy. She looked utterly miserable, and she knew then that she just could not feel right again without Cole in her life. She would do whatever she had to to get him back.

Now, as students continued to rush from one class to the next, Stacie continued to look hopefully for Cole's face among the crowds.

A moment later, she saw him, heading her way. Soon, he was standing right before her. "What are you doing here?" he said, not seeming all that happy to see her.

"I need to talk to you."

"You've already done that," Cole said, stepping beside her to open his locker door. "There ain't nothing left to say."

"But there is. Last night I couldn't get to sleep. I cried all night thinking about us not being together anymore."

"So?" Cole said, slamming his locker door shut.

"So?" Stacie echoed, scarcely believing that Cole could act this way toward her. "I love you. That means something. We have a relationship together."

"You love me?" Cole said, louder than Stacie felt he had to. "If you loved me so much, why did you dump me?"

"Cole," Stacie said, lowering her voice. "I only did that because I was afraid you'd find somebody else to . . . you know."

"But I told you I wouldn't. I told you!" Cole said, getting louder.

Stacie noticed that they were catching the attention of passing students. A few had even stopped in the hall to listen to what they were saying.

"Cole, can we go somewhere private and talk?"

"No. You came to my locker to talk about it. Let's talk about it," Cole said, gesturing widely with his arms. "You say we had a relationship that meant something."

"That's right," Stacie said, as the crowd grew even larger.

"If we had such a good relationship, then what's been going on in my life the past three days?"

Stacie looked at Cole, not sure what he was talking about. She hadn't expected to be quizzed. "I don't know. Besides the stuff with us?"

Cole shook his head. "That's what I'm talking about. If you loved me so much, if we had such a good relationship, you'd know that I found my father after three years. I thought he might be coming home, but now it looks like that's never gonna happen."

Stacie felt awful. "Oh, Cole . . . I'm so sorry. . . . I had no idea." She tried to give him a hug, but he put his hands up to stop her.

"Thanks for being sorry," Cole said. "But it would've been nice if while I was dealing with all that, the person I thought was my girl, the person I thought really loved me, could've supported me, been there for me. Instead, she tells me that she's done with me."

"Let me try and make it right, Cole," Stacie begged, tears coming to her eyes.

"I think it's a little too late for that," Cole said, turning and pushing his way through the crowd that had surrounded them.

"Cole, stop!" Stacie yelled. But the bell announcing the next period drowned her voice out.

Chapter Seventeen

COLE GOT HOME late after practice that night. The house was mostly dark and quiet. He headed to his mother's room and knocked softly on the door.

"Come in," he heard her say.

He pushed the door open and entered the dark room. A moment later, the bedside lamp came on; his mother was slowly sitting up in bed, a sleeping scarf around her hair.

"Did you see your father today?" Lana asked, barely awake.

"Yeah, his ego was still a little bruised, but I think he's gonna be okay."

"We'll have to have him back over for dinner soon."

"Won't Edric have something to say about that?" Cole asked.

"It doesn't matter anymore what Edric has to say. After the way he showed out, I'm not dealing with his ass any longer. I called him over, gave him back his tiny engagement ring, and told him never to call me again."

"You go, Ma!" Cole said, leaning against the doorframe.

"Yeah, I thought you'd appreciate that. Now, go on to bed. Some people have work early in the morning."

"Love you, Ma," Cole said, smiling, pulling the door closed.

"I love you, too," he heard his mother say.

Cole walked into his room and softly closed his door; kicking off his shoes, he climbed into bed. He clicked on the TV, surfed through a few dozen channels, then gave up and clicked it off.

He stripped down to his boxers, reached over and turned off his bedside lamp, and was preparing to turn in for the night, when his cell phone started to vibrate.

He picked it up. The caller ID said it was Donesha calling.

"What's up, Donesha? It's after eleven o'clock. Is everything cool with Stacie?" Cole asked, instinctively concerned.

"Yeah, everything's cool with her, I guess. Nothing's new."

Cole settled into his bed. "I guess she told you what happened between us, then."

"Naw, she ain't say anything to me. I was just calling to see if you found your father. But what happened between the two of y'all?"

Cole found it odd that Stacie hadn't mentioned anything to Donesha, but he guessed the breakup wasn't affecting her as badly as it was him. He told Donesha what had happened. "I guess I was wrong for pressuring her, huh?"

There was no response for a long moment.

"Donesha, you there?"

"Yeah, I'm here, Cole. I just don't know if you want to hear what I really think about the situation."

"Of course I do."

"If a woman loves a man, then she should show him. That's what I think. I know if I was in a relationship with a man I loved, I wouldn't have a problem showing him."

"You wouldn't?" Cole said.

"No," Donesha said, her voice softening just a little. "He could do whatever he wanted to me. You know?"

"Uh-huh."

"I mean, if I was in a relationship with a man—take, for instance, you—I would let you come over here right now, and I'd let you come up in my room."

"For real?" Cole said, not sure exactly what was happening, but allowing it to continue regardless.

"That's right," Donesha said, her voice becoming still softer, more sultry. "And as you stood across the room, I'd

{ 114 }

ask if you wanted me to take off my clothes. And when you said yes, I would slowly undo my bra, and then I'd turn around, bend over my bed, and slowly take off everything else."

Cole started to breathe hard, feeling himself become excited against his will.

"And then, I'd get on all fours and walk over to you like a pussycat. Would you like that, Cole?"

Cole didn't answer right away. When he finally did, it came out more like a grunt than an answer.

Donesha laughed a little, her voice sounding sexier than Cole would've ever imagined it. "Baby, you know I miss you, don't you?"

"Yeah," Cole said, his head spinning with lust.

"And you know you can have me whenever you want. You know that, right?"

"Yeah . . . I mean, no, I can't," Cole heard himself say. He could barely think. Donesha was getting him highly aroused. Not necessarily her, specifically, because he still loved Stacie, but the temptation, the experience, the thought of losing his virginity.

"You can come and get it now, baby, if you want it. My mother's asleep. She won't hear you come in."

Cole thought about it, saw himself throwing on his clothes, driving over there, and getting down with Donesha. "No," he said. "I'm sorry, but I can't. I have to go."

"Are you sure, Cole?"

He wasn't. Not at all. "Yeah. I'm sure." He hung up the phone before he could change his mind.

The following day, Cole couldn't bring himself to go to school, mostly because he couldn't face Donesha after what had happened on the phone with her the previous night. He felt dirty, as though he had committed some betrayal against Stacie.

That was foolish, he thought, as he watched a football game on ESPN. Stacie had dumped him. What difference would it have made if he had actually gone over to Donesha's house?

Cole's mother walked in at five, carrying several grocery bags. "How was school today?"

"I didn't go. I wasn't feeling well."

"You didn't miss any—"

"No, Ma . . ." Cole said, anticipating her question. "I didn't miss any tests, and Tony is getting all my home-work."

"Good." Lana walked into the kitchen and started putting away the groceries.

Cole walked in after her, his hands behind his back. "Ma, I was bored with my room, so I was watching TV in your bed today. I hope you don't mind."

"As long as you weren't eating in there," his mother said, sticking a box of cookies on one of the cabinet shelves.

"Uh, there's something else. I found something, and

I was hoping you could tell me what it is."

Cole's mother turned to her son. "Found what?"

Cole smiled and pulled a yellowed, dog-eared sheet of notebook paper from behind his back. "I found a letter written to you back on—" Cole read the date—"February fourteenth, 1987."

Lana practically ran across the kitchen. "Give me that. That's why I need to start locking my door."

"That's a letter from Dad, isn't it?"

"It was the first letter he ever sent me. We were juniors in high school. We had been dating for six months, and your father wanted to, well, take it to the next level. I told him it was too soon. We went back and forth, trying to come to some conclusion about what was right for us, but when we couldn't, it seemed that we were going to break up for sure. We stopped talking for almost a week, and then one day, one of my girlfriends gave me this letter and said it was from your father. He said that he didn't want to lose me. He said he realized it would happen when it was meant to, and regardless of how long that took, he would wait. And then he wrote that he loved me."

Cole's mother held the letter out for Cole to see the words on the page.

"It was the first time he said those words to me," Lana said wistfully. "He was a good man then."

"He's still a good man," Cole said. "He just needs another chance."

"Cole, please don't start with that again," his mother said, folding the letter and placing it in a drawer.

"You can't tell me you haven't thought about him since the other night."

"No, Cole. I haven't."

"That's not true, or you wouldn't have dug out that letter. Ma, I've been cooped up in this house all day. Let's go see him."

"Where? On the street?" Lana said.

"That wasn't nice, Ma. Pops isn't homeless anymore."

"I know. I'm sorry."

"There's a lot you don't know about him. He works a job; he has a small place to himself. He's even about to finish his first semester of college."

"Get out," Lana said.

"For real. Let's just go and see him, Ma. He can tell you himself how good he's been doing."

His mother seemed to be considering it for a moment, but then she shook her head sadly and said, "Cole, the man is still an addict. I don't want to go getting all hopeful, only to have him turn around and—"

"He's been clean for six months, Ma. He's cured."

"Cole, an addict is never cured. If you only knew how long it took for me to get past the hurt of putting him out, of taking your father away from you. I don't want to have to go through something like that again."

"Ma," Cole begged, tugging on her arm. "You won't. I promise. Come with me, and I'll show you."

Forty-five minutes later, Cole walked into the reception area of the halfway house where Franklin lived. Lana walked in behind him.

"Excuse me," Cole said to a tall blond man behind the check-in desk. "We're here to see Mr. Franklin Stevens. I'm his son," Cole said, smiling, "and this is his wife, Mrs. Stevens," Cole said, nodding to his mother.

"Cole," Lana warned.

"Just a moment," the man said, thumbing through a Rolodex. The tall man—Mr. Reynolds, according to his name tag—plucked a card from the wheel, examined it, and again said, "Just a moment." He stood up from his chair and walked to the back of the reception area, where two other staff people stood.

Cole looked at his mother, who shot a confused look right back at him.

When Mr. Reynolds came back to the desk, Cole asked, "Is everything all right?"

"I'm sorry, but I thought it was Mr. Stevens they came for last night."

"Who came for?" Lana asked, stepping up to the desk.

"The ambulance. There was an incident. One of your husband's neighbors found him unconscious in his room, and the paramedics were called."

"Is he okay?" Cole asked, getting a little scared.

"I'm sorry. All I can tell you is that they took him to John H. Stroger Jr. Hospital."

* * *

As the attending physician walked Cole and Lana to Franklin's room in the intensive care unit, he explained to them that Franklin had overdosed on heroin. He wasn't sure of the exact amount he had injected into his system, but it had been enough to put him into a coma.

Cole's mother came to a halt right in the middle of the hallway.

"Coma?" Her eyes showed genuine concern. "When will he wake up?"

"To be honest with you, there's no telling. We've given him an MRI, and his scans look normal. He could wake up any moment," the doctor said. "Then again, there's a chance he may not wake up at all."

Cole had been sitting at his father's bedside for the better part of an hour. He stared at his father's peaceful face; Franklin's eyes were closed; the white blankets were pulled up to his chest. He looked as if he were just sleeping. Cole held his father's hand, willing him to open his eyes.

Cole felt his mother hovering somewhere behind him, and he knew she was probably asking herself a million questions at that moment.

"Why won't he just wake up?"

"He can't," Lana replied.

"He looks like all he's doing is sleeping."

"Well, he's not just sleeping. He's in a coma." Cole

recognized a trace of anger in his mother's voice.

Lana turned and took a few steps away from him, raking her fingers through her hair.

She walked to the opposite side of the hospital bed, looked down at Cole's father, and sighed as she shook her head.

"And you wonder why I put him out," she said. "I knew this would happen one day. I just knew it. I got rid of him because I didn't want to be around to see it, didn't want you to have to see it, Cole. But somehow, he managed to pull it off when we were around. Like he held off, waited for just this moment."

"He didn't plan it, Ma," Cole said, in defense of his father. "He was trying to beat it."

"I guess he didn't try hard enough," Lana said, her eyes beginning to water again. "And I was just starting to believe what you were saying about him, too. I thought there might have been the slightest chance that he actually would give up the drugs, and maybe, just maybe, we could've tried again. And then he does this. I'll never let myself think that again."

"Ma, you can't stop believing that. You can't stop loving him. He needs us."

Lana wiped her eyes with the back of her hand and said, "I still love your father, Cole. The problem is he doesn't love us anymore. If he did, he would've never let this happen."

"He didn't mean for this to happen, Ma."

"Come on, it's time to go."

Cole grabbed his father's arm with both hands. "You go, I'm staying."

"Dammit, Cole!" Lana said, raising her voice. "I said, we're leaving."

Cole sat there, staring up at his mother, realizing that she must've been as hurt as he was. He almost wished he had never suggested going out there to see his father.

After a moment, the expression on Lana's face softened, and she said, "Okay, ten more minutes, and then we have to go."

She leaned over and kissed Cole on the cheek, then left him alone with his father.

Chapter Eighteen

STACIE SAT across from her father at the dining room table, staring at the Scrabble board between them.

She watched halfheartedly as her father lay five of his seven wooden tiles down on the board with a triumphant flourish. "Double-letter score, *and* triple-word score. Beat that." He picked up the pencil and scribbled down his points.

Stacie just continued to stare blankly at the board, her elbows on the table, her chin cupped in her hands.

"What's up? Your turn," Clark said.

"I'm done."

"But it's still a close game."

"You win," Stacie said, tossing her letters back into the bag.

"Fine," her father said. "But if we aren't going to play, you're going to talk to me."

"Nothing to talk about," Stacie said glumly.

"Oh, yes, there is. You've been moping around this house for the past few days. I want to know what's going on," Clark said, pushing the game aside.

"No, Dad. I don't really think you do want to know what's going on."

"Try me."

"Fine," Stacie said, unfolding her legs from beneath her and sitting up straight in her chair. "You want to know what I've been thinking about? I've been thinking about what would happen if I had sex with Cole."

Her father coughed, cleared his throat, and stared at the ceiling, as if trying to properly digest what he'd just heard.

"And I don't mean stuff like getting grounded, never being able to see him again, you wanting to kill him. I know all that stuff," Stacie continued. "I mean the real bad stuff. The reasons why fathers get so hung up about their daughters having sex."

"Okay," Clark finally said, seeming to have recovered from his initial shock. "This is hypothetical, correct? You aren't planning on having sex with him, are you?"

"No. I'm just asking."

"Very well, then, there's the risk of STDs."

"But what if you're safe? Can't you use protection?"

"There's still the risk."

"In sex ed, the teacher said when used properly, condoms are, like, ninety-nine percent effective."

"Well, there's still that one percent you have to watch out for," Clark said. "And then there's pregnancy."

"Again," Stacie said. "Condom."

"They can break."

"But what if they don't?"

"Would you want to take that chance?" Clark asked.

"I'm sure you did, didn't you, Dad?"

Clark looked as though he were thinking about answering the question, but then he said, "What is this all about, anyway? Why are you asking me these questions?"

Stacie paused for a moment, considering whether or not to tell her father the truth. "I just broke up with my boyfriend, who I really loved, and I'm trying to figure out why I did." She felt the weight of her sorrow well up inside as she continued to look at her father for answers; the tears were about to spill over.

"Aw, sweetheart," Clark said, reaching out and taking her hand in his.

"Dad, I'm almost seventeen years old. And it's going to happen one day. We both know it. Is it that you just don't want me living in your house when it does? Is it that you don't think any boy is good enough? What is it?" Stacie asked, sobbing now.

Her father got up, walked around the table, and sat down again beside Stacie; he wrapped his arms around her.

"Sweetheart," he said, kissing her head, "it's all of those things and none of those things. But even though you're almost seventeen, you're still young. Sex is not just physical. Your heart gets involved, more than you could ever imagine. And if you start having sex, and Cole decides he doesn't want to be with you anymore, you're going to hurt ten times more than you're hurting now. A thousand times more."

"But Cole wouldn't do that. He wouldn't break up with me if we were to have sex. He loves me," Stacie said, wiping her eyes.

"Stacie, I hate to say this. But if he truly loved you, he'd wait until you're ready."

Chapter Nineteen

THE NEXT EVENING after school, Cole stopped by the hospital to visit his father.

He got to the room and sat by the bed, holding Franklin's hand, looking for long stretches of time at his eyelids, hoping to see a hint of movement.

There was none.

After an hour, Cole stood up, leaned over his father, and kissed him on the forehead. "I'll be back tomorrow, Pops," he said. See you then."

When he got home and walked into the kitchen, he could hear the TV going in the living room.

He stepped in and saw his mother sitting on the couch.

He sat down with her, his shoulders slumped, a sad expression on his face.

Lana glanced at him. "What's wrong?"

"Stuff."

"Did you visit your father?"

"No change," Cole said.

"Don't worry. He's strong. He'll be okay."

"I know, but I guess that's not what's really bothering me."

"What's up?" Lana asked, scooting a little closer to him.

Cole looked at his mother, then glanced at the sitcom playing on the TV screen.

"You mind if I turn this down some?" he asked, grabbing the remote.

"You can turn it off."

Cole clicked off the TV and set the remote back down. "It's about Stacie."

Cole told his mother everything. About how they'd been dealing with sex in the relationship, how he might have been pressuring her to have sex, how she hadn't wanted to at first, and then how she had changed her mind. Without going into too much detail, he told his mother how horrible things had turned out the night they'd tried, and then how things had just seemed to get worse ever since. Once he got started, Cole found that the words tumbled out; he hadn't realized how much it would help to talk things out with someone. He told his mother how Stacie had broken up with him, then tried to say she wanted him back.

"I don't know what's going on, Ma. You really think she doesn't love me anymore?"

"Cole," his mother said, "I know that's not the case. She was scared, as we all are our first time. Maybe she just wants a little time out to get ahold of her feelings. Or maybe she even thinks that you don't want to be with her. You were the one who brought up the idea of being with someone else."

"I know, but I didn't really mean that."

"Well, you never should've said it."

"I know," Cole said, "but what am I supposed to do now?"

"Just talk to her."

"I did, at school, when she tried to make up with me," Cole said, remembering the guilt he had felt. "I went off on her pretty bad, in front of, like, a bunch a people. I don't think she'll want to hear what I have to say now."

Lana smiled a little as she looked at her son.

"Ma, it's not funny," Cole said.

"I know it's not. I'm sorry. It's just so adorable. You really love that girl, don't you?"

"Yeah, Ma. I do. So how do I handle this?"

His mother gave it a moment of thought, then said, "It seems as though kids don't do this anymore, with you all carrying cell phones and having e-mail and stuff, but you could do what your father did. You could write her a letter."

"A letter?" Cole said. The idea sounded so retro . . . and a bit corny.

"I know what you're thinking, but you'd probably be surprised by the effect a well-worded letter can have on a girl."

"Really?" Cole said.

"Well, let me put it this way. Your father wrote me that letter when I was sixteen, and I still have it."

Cole sat in his car, which was parked outside Donesha's house. He had been waiting for about ten minutes; he kept looking up at her window to see if she was coming.

He'd called Donesha half an hour earlier to tell her he was coming over, so that she could look out for him, but she had obviously forgotten.

He dialed her number on his cell phone and waited for her to pick up.

"Hello?" Donesha said.

"I'm out front. You were supposed to be watching for me," Cole said, still looking up at the window.

"Oh, I see you."

Cole saw her head pop into view.

"Why don't you come on up?" Donesha said.

"No. I told you, I'm not here to talk. I got something I need to give to you."

"All right, all right. I'll be right down."

Cole closed his phone and slid it back into his pocket.

He would have to set things straight with Donesha. Although he'd once liked her, what had happened on the phone the other night had been a mistake. He knew he never should've let her get him worked up like that, putting him on the verge of doing something he would never have forgiven himself for.

Cole looked up when he heard the front door open and saw Donesha come trotting down the walkway, wearing skintight spandex shorts, a halter top, and flip-flops.

Cole turned away, but he hadn't been able to avoid noticing how firm her body looked.

As Donesha opened the passenger-side door and slid into the seat, Cole grabbed the envelope that was sitting on the dashboard.

He had done as his mother suggested and written a letter to Stacie to explain all the emotions he had been feeling.

"Hey," Donesha said, smiling seductively. Her hair had just been styled. "Give me a hug."

Cole reluctantly obliged with a brief embrace, pulling away quickly.

"It's after ten, man," Donesha said. "What's going on?"

"I want to give you this." Cole held the sealed envelope out to her; Stacie's name was written in big block letters across the front of it.

Donesha looked at it. "I thought you guys broke up. Why you writing her?"

"We did break up. But there are some things I need to tell her."

"You could've just called me, and I would've—"

"I don't think she's talking to me. Besides, the letter explains it better. Will you give it to her tomorrow for me?"

Donesha ran a fingertip across the top edge of the envelope. "Sure." She smiled sweetly and added, "Have you given any more thought to what happened the other night?"

Cole was already starting the engine of his car. He had no intention of discussing the other night with Donesha at that moment.

"Donesha, I got to be going," Cole said, turning the music up. "Just give her the letter for me, okay?"

"Okay," Donesha said, looking slighted. She jumped out of the car. Cole didn't even wait till she made it to her porch before driving off.

Chapter Twenty

ONCE INSIDE the house, Donesha hurried up the stairs to her bedroom, locked her door behind her, and threw herself on the bed, giddiness filling her entire body.

She flopped onto her back, holding the letter high above her.

"Stacie." She read aloud the name printed on the back.

Giggling gleefully, Donesha stuck one of her fake nails into the fold of the letter and easily ripped it open.

She snatched out the pages, unfolded them, and counted them: there were three in all. They were neatly typed out, double-spaced, with an inch-and-a-half margin all around.

"Got a lot to say, huh, Mr. Cole?" Donesha said, setting her eyes upon the first two words and reading them aloud.

"Dear Stacie."

It took her fifteen minutes to read the entire letter.

The boy should've been a novelist, Donesha thought. He sure can tell a good story. She laughed to herself.

Cole started the letter talking about the day he had first seen Stacie. He described how he was scared to go up to her at first, and then how he'd finally found his nerve and said hi, and how his life had never been the same since.

He talked about how he had fallen in love with Stacie, how his friends had teased him and pressured him to push her to have sex. Cole wrote that he should have had a mind of his own, but that his friends' influence over him, and his own love for Stacie, had made him continue to pester her.

He understood if Stacie wasn't ready to have sex, the letter said. They could wait until she was completely comfortable, because the last thing he wanted to do was lose her.

The words *I love you* must have appeared about fifty times in the letter. If Donesha hadn't found it all sickeningly sappy, she probably would've been touched, as she was sure Stacie would've been.

Cole even discussed his father's situation, explaining Franklin's drug addiction to Stacie, detailing the episode when his mom threw Franklin out on the street, and then going into his life as a homeless man and his current admission to the hospital after his overdose.

Donesha read that last part over slowly. She did genuinely care what happened to Mr. Stevens. He had always been nice to her.

At that moment, she felt sorry for Cole. She felt it was a shame that he was going through all this with his father and that his girlfriend wasn't there to comfort him, give him what he needed.

But Donesha would make sure Cole would never have to beg Stacie again for what he wanted, because she was ready to give it to him now; she had always been ready.

When she was finished with the letter, Donesha hopped out of bed, went to her desk, and turned on her computer.

Stacie would get a letter from Cole, Donesha thought. Just not the one he had written.

Chapter Twenty-One

"**D**ADDY AND I had a talk last night," Stacie said, looking over at her sister, Mya. It was Saturday morning, and the two were sitting in Mya's kitchen. Tiffany sat in her high chair, allowing her mother to spoon baby food into her mouth.

"About what?" Mya said, scooping some of the food off Mya's chin and pushing it back between the infant's lips.

"About me having sex with Cole."

"What?" Mya said, almost dropping the spoon in shock.

"It wasn't anything weird or crazy like that. I was asking Daddy what's the big deal about it."

"And he said he doesn't want you to get pregnant like me."

"He didn't say 'like you,' but, yeah, he doesn't want me to get pregnant, or catch a disease, or get emotionally hurt."

"Whatever," Mya said, screwing the top back on to the baby-food jar. "So, you done with Cole for good now, or what?"

"No," Stacie said. "I thought about everything, and I'm not ready to give him up. I still want to be with him—that is, if he still wants to be with me."

"That boy eats and sleeps you, Stacie. You two just need to talk things out, and you'll be fine."

Stacie smiled, blushing. "You think?"

"Yeah."

"I hope so," Stacie said. Then she carefully changed the subject. "I also talked to Daddy about when he was going to let you come."

"Stacie, I told you not to ask him anything about me," Mya scolded. "He's not ever letting me come home."

"He didn't say that."

"Then what did he say?"

"He didn't want to talk about it," Stacie said, reaching over and grabbing one of Tiffany's little hands. "But you need to just go over there one day and tell him you're coming back. Bring your bags. I'll help you with Tiff, and you just move back in. Forget him. Who is he to say you can't go back?"

"Uh, just the owner of the house. And I told you a thousand times," Mya said, "I don't need to move back there. I'm fine right here. Everything is cool. I've got my own place. I can come and go as I please, and I kinda like it here."

Stacie looked around at the peeling paint on the walls, the stains on the carpet, the cracks in the windows. "You like it here? Really? Look, why can't we just get your things and have you come home?"

"I told you, everything's fine, and I'm not going nowhere."

Just then, a knock came at the front door.

"Watch her," Mya said, getting up and hurrying to the door.

Stacie scooted her chair a little closer to her niece. She poked Tiff softly in the belly; the baby smiled and giggled.

Stacie heard a man's voice at the front door. "I don't want to hear it. That's what you said last month."

"Can you keep it down? I don't need my business out on the street," Stacie heard Mya say, her voice hushed.

Stacie pulled Tiff out of her high chair, cradled the baby in her arms, and walked to the kitchen door, trying to hear what was going on.

"Ms. Winston," the man said, "I have not received rent for last month, or the month before that, and you're late again."

"I told you, I'm going to get it to you. It's just that—"

"No excuses. I'm tired of them," the man said, in a louder voice.

"Please, just give me two more weeks. I promise—"

Stacie heard Mya plead, but the man would not listen.

"So, you don't have the money?"

"No," Mya said, sounding exasperated. "If I did, I would give it to you."

"Then I have no choice but to start the eviction process. Good-bye, Ms. Winston."

"But Mr. Brown, please, just—"

"Good-bye, Ms. Winston," Stacie heard the man say again; then she heard the sound of his heavy footsteps fading away.

There was silence for a long moment. Stacie did not move from the wall, where she stood holding Tiffany. She remained there, waiting for her sister.

For a few moments, nothing happened. Finally, Stacie heard the front door close. She overheard her sister sniffling, and when Mya walked back into the kitchen, she could tell that her sister had been trying to hide her tears.

"Mya, please—" Stacie said.

Mya cut her off, tears in her eyes, holding up one finger. "Like I said, I don't want his help, and I'm not going nowhere."

Mya told Stacie she wanted to be alone for a little while, so Stacie went over to Donesha's house. She wasn't ready to be alone at home, and her sister's situation was making her feel particularly angry toward her father.

She sat with Donesha in the living room, drinking sodas, watching TV, the volume turned down.

She told Donesha everything that had just happened with Mya.

"So, you think your father is going to let her come back?" Donesha asked.

"I don't know. But I got to do something. That's just not right."

"I know, girl," Donesha said, looking at Stacie strangely.

Stacie tried to ignore her friend's gaze. She tried to focus on the TV, but she kept feeling Donesha's eyes on her face.

"What?" she said finally.

"Nothin'. I'm just surprised you ain't said nothing about Cole."

"I guess I have nothing to say. I'm not going to think anything more negative about it. I'm just telling myself that I know he loves me as much as I love him, and that we're going to get back together, no matter what."

"Really?" Donesha said, raising her eyebrows.

"That's right. What, you don't believe me?"

"Of course I do," Donesha said, rising from the sofa. "In fact, I think I got something here that you might want to see."

"What are you talking about?" Stacie said, watching Donesha curiously.

Donesha walked over to the bookcase and pulled an envelope from one of the shelves. She held it out for Stacie.

"What is it?" Stacie asked.

"It's a letter from Cole."

"For me?"

"Uh, it says *Stacie* on it, so I guess it's for you."

Stacie took the envelope from Donesha and held it, her hands slightly trembling. "I wonder what it says."

"Open it. I'm sure it'll tell you."

"But what if it's a Dear Jane letter?"

"You two are already supposed to be broken up. He can't do it again," Donesha said. "He's probably trying to get back together with you. Open it and see."

"No," Stacie said, pressing the letter to her chest. "I'm going to go home, and read it, then call you and tell you what it says."

"Okay, girl. Suit yourself," Donesha said.

Chapter Twenty-Two

DONESHA SAT on the living room sofa and watched through the window as Stacie descended the front steps and quickly walked away from her house, the letter grasped carefully in her right hand.

She had wanted Stacie to open it and read it right there in front of her, to see the expression on her face go from hopeful to hopeless. She was prepared to do the whole "best friend" dance, consoling Stacie while she cried her eyes out, all the while taking pleasure in the fact that Cole would soon be hers. But Stacie had robbed her of that.

Donesha watched Stacie till she was out of sight, then turned around on the sofa, threw her head back, and stretched her arms across the back of the couch as she got ready to put the next phase of her plan into action.

While she was writing the "letter from Cole," Donesha had realized that she might succeed in hurting Stacie briefly. But then she'd thought of what would happen after the letter was read.

Stacie would somehow contact Cole. Cole would tell Stacie that the letter she had seen wasn't the same letter he had given Donesha, and Donesha would be found out. It would have been a very short-lived victory.

No, Donesha thought, quickly getting up from the sofa. The game wasn't over yet. She had more damage to do. She ran upstairs to her room, closed the door, grabbed her cell phone from the dresser, then sat on the edge of her bed.

She punched in Stacie's phone number, hoping that Stacie's father was home.

"Hello?" Clark answered.

"Hi, Mr. Winston," Donesha said, putting on her sweetest voice. "May I speak to Stacie, please?"

"I'm sorry, she's not home. May I ask who's calling?"

"Can you just tell her Donesha called?"

"Oh, hi, Donesha. Yeah, sure thing. I'll tell her. Good-bye."

"I mean—" Donesha continued before Clark could hang up. "I haven't seen or spoken to her in, like, a week, and I was just starting to worry."

Donesha heard silence on the other end for a moment,

then smiled as Stacie's father said, "But didn't you and Stacie go to the movies a few nights ago?"

"Oh," Donesha said, pausing for dramatic effect. "Uh, yeah. Uh, that's right. We did, ummm . . ."

"Donesha," Clark said, his voice firm. "Did you or did you not go to the movies with Stacie the other night?"

"Oh, ummm . . . you know what? Never mind, I shouldn't have called. Stacie's going to be so mad at me if she finds out."

"Donesha, calm down. Just tell me the truth. I won't tell Stacie I heard this from you."

"Do you promise, Mr. Winston?" Donesha purred. "This was supposed to be our secret."

"I promise. I won't let her know you told me. Did she go to the movies with you the other night?"

"No, Mr. Winston. I don't know where she was, but she wasn't with me."

Chapter Twenty-Three

WHEN STACIE walked in the front door of her house, she was sobbing uncontrollably; the letter that she had gotten from Donesha was crumpled in her left hand.

On the bus ride home, the envelope had sat on Stacie's lap, tempting her every so often to open and read it. She'd forced herself to focus her attention outside the window, so that she could wait until she got home to read the letter. She'd resisted until she made it to her stop. After getting off the bus, she'd lost whatever control she had and quickly tore open the envelope.

As she pulled out the letter, she had told herself

that maybe it wouldn't be bad. Maybe Cole was taking a different approach to communicating with her. Maybe he had some nice things to say; maybe he was even apologizing for yelling at her in front of everybody at school.

Stacie had unfolded the single page and started reading. Immediately she'd frowned, her grip tightening on the page.

Cole's letter had pierced right through her heart. It said that he'd been thinking of trying to give them a second chance, but then realized it was truly over between them. He said that he was sorry for making the mistake of being with her in the first place, and that the first time she'd turned him down about having sex should've been the last. According to the letter, he had thought that she loved him, but obviously she didn't even know what love was, or she would have shown him by now.

Stacie's teary eyes had just skimmed over the rest of the words on the page, because they all basically said the same thing: Cole wanted nothing more to do with her ever again.

The last words on the page told her not to call him anymore, and not to approach him at school, because he was done talking about it. He wanted to be alone, to start a new relationship as soon as he possibly could, so that he could stop being a virgin and start making up for all the sex he had been missing while he was with her.

Now Stacie thought about those words as she climbed

the stairs, her head down, the crumpled letter still in her grasp.

If she had only had sex with him that night in the hotel, Stacie thought, this wouldn't be happening. But she hadn't, because she was so worried about what her father thought. Laying in the hotel bed, all she had seen was her father's face, judging her, watching her.

But wasn't he the one who'd told her that if he had only given her mother what she wanted, she probably wouldn't have left him?

Why hadn't Stacie paid more attention to that? Why hadn't she learned from her father's mistakes?

It's all his fault, Stacie told herself as she climbed the last step in the stairway. She turned toward her room and then froze, hearing a noise from behind her bedroom door.

She listened again, thinking that maybe it was her imagination. But then she heard it again. There was no mistake. She'd definitely heard something.

No, it can't be, Stacie told herself, rushing toward her room. He wouldn't dare do it again.

She pushed the door wide open, and it banged against the wall, startling her father, who was hunched over in her closet.

Stacie couldn't believe her eyes, she just couldn't. She felt as if she were having déjà vu.

"What are you doing?" Stacie practically screamed.

"Where have *you* been?" her father said, half turning to her from inside the closet.

"What are you doing in my room?" Stacie said, even louder this time.

"I said, where have you been?"

"I went to Mya's, then Donesha's. I told you that!"

"Don't lie to me," her father said. "We were supposed to have trust. You've been lying to me."

"Who are you to talk about trust? You said you would never—"

"Where did you go the other night when you were supposed to be at the movies? Were you with that boy Cole?"

Even the mention of Cole's name now hurt her. She couldn't talk about him.

"Get out of my room!" Stacie screamed.

"I'm not leaving till you tell me what's going on. You've been acting strangely, always in your room, depressed. And then the questions about sex you asked me the other night."

Stacie couldn't believe she had sacrificed everything with Cole, trying to do right by her father, and for what? For him still to mistrust her and rummage through her stuff?

"Tell me what's going on, Stacie," her father said. "Are you having sex with that boy?"

"No. I'm telling you the truth!"

"Then what's this?" her father asked, pulling the lingerie Stacie had bought from Victoria's Secret out of the closet. "If there's nothing going on, why do you need these?"

That was the last straw. Her father didn't trust her at all; seeing him standing there with her underwear hanging from his fingers was just way too much for Stacie.

"Answer me," he said, walking toward her. "Are you trying to have sex with this boy even though I told you not to? Because if you are—"

"No, Daddy. I'm not *trying* to have sex with him," Stacie said. All she could think about was how much her father was hurting her. "I already did! And it was good. We did it three times," Stacie spat, full of rage, the same rage she now saw building in her father. "And we didn't even use anything. Who knows, I might even be pregnant right now."

That last statement provoked her father to raise his hand, as if getting ready to slap her.

Stacie turned away. She tightened her face preparing for the slap, but it never came.

When she opened her eyes, she saw that her father had managed to hold back.

It didn't matter. The damage had already been done. The pain of his striking her could never be worse than the betrayal of his going back on his word to her.

They stood there, face to face, for a second that seemed like forever.

Stacie saw regret begin to creep over her father's face.

But before he could say anything else, she turned and ran as fast as she could out of the room, down the stairs, and out the front door.

Her father gave chase, but she would not let him catch her. She ran toward the neighbor's house, quickly hopped the fence, ran through the yard, and continued running, never looking back.

She heard her father calling her name, but the longer she ran, the fainter his calls became.

Chapter Twenty-Four

"COME ON, COLE," Lana said, gently squeezing his arm, attempting to ease him away from his father's hospital bed.

"I thought I saw his eye move. It was just a little bit, but I thought I saw it," Cole said in a wistful tone.

"We've been here two hours. If your father wakes up while we're gone, the doctor has promised to call us. You know that." Cole's mother turned him around to face her. "We'll be the first ones here to visit him. I promise."

"I know, Ma," Cole said glumly. He turned to his father and leaned over to kiss him on the forehead. That had become Cole's daily ritual. "I'll see you later, Pops." He was about to turn back toward his mother when again he thought he saw his father's eyelid flutter just a little.

Cole told himself that his imagination was making him see things that he wanted to see. But a second later, he saw it again. There was now no question in his mind.

"Ma!" Cole called, yanking his mother's hand. "Dad's eyes, they're moving. See?"

Lana rushed to the side of the bed. "You're right!"

"He's waking up, Ma," Cole said, thrilled, as he watched his father's eyes move more rapidly, then saw his hands start to move.

"Pops!" Cole called, clasping his father's hands in his. Suddenly, his mother grabbed him.

"Hold it, Cole," Lana warned.

Franklin's hands now moved even more, twitching frantically, the movement spreading up to his arms, then his neck, until his head was whipping back and forth across the pillow.

"Ma, what's wrong?" Cole cried.

"Oh, Lord!" Lana screamed, as the bedside monitors started to flash and beep loudly around them. "Call a doctor, Cole! Quick, get somebody." Lana pushed Cole toward the door. "Your father's having a seizure!"

"Your husband is stable," a brown-skinned woman with salt-and-pepper hair was saying. Cole sat beside his mother in the waiting room, his face in his hands.

"What caused it, Doctor?" Lana asked.

"He's getting scanned right now. We won't know till we do some tests, and I don't want to speculate until we have the results."

"Will my father be all right?" Cole asked.

"He'll be fine," Lana said, stroking his hair.

Cole pulled away. "No," he said, visibly upset. "I want to know the truth. Will my father be all right? Will he wake up?"

"To be perfectly honest, Cole," the doctor said, "I don't know." She turned to Cole's mother. "Go home. Get some rest. It's going to be a long night for everyone. Doesn't make sense to spend it here. We'll call you the moment we know something."

Cole was silent throughout the entire ride home.

His mother pulled into the driveway and parked the car. She turned to Cole and said, "You can have anything you want for dinner. I can cook, we can go out, delivery—whatever."

"I'm not hungry, Ma. I just need to get out for a while, take a drive. Can I?"

"Sure." Lana reached out her arms to Cole; he leaned forward, laying his head on her shoulder. "Just keep your cell phone on so I can contact you, in case something happens."

"Okay. Love you, Ma."

"Love you, too."

Chapter Twenty-Five

ON THE WAY OVER, Cole knew he was doing something crazy. He knew her father would've been fine with never seeing Cole again. But he had to see Stacie.

When he had seen his father thrashing around on the hospital bed, when he had realized that he might lose him that very moment, the only thing Cole could think was that he wished Stacie were there by his side.

Regardless of what Stacie's father had to say, Cole knew he had to see his girlfriend. He needed to tell her that he didn't give a damn about sex, about what people thought, about any of that. He loved her, and that was all that mattered.

He had put that in the letter he had given to Donesha. She'd said she would get it to Stacie as soon as possible, and Cole had been waiting for Stacie to call.

He figured she would forgive him as soon as she'd read what he had written to her. But it seemed he was wrong.

That doesn't matter now, Cole told himself, pulling his car to a stop in front of Stacie's house, where a single light burned in the front room.

He climbed out of his car and slowly walked up the path leading to the house. He decided he would be brave, firm, but respectful. He would tell her father why he was there and what he wanted to say, and then, before leaving, he would make Stacie understand that he never wanted to spend another day without her again.

Cole rang the doorbell.

He didn't realize how nervous he would be. He turned and looked back at his car, not knowing why.

Trying to calm himself he turned back around and saw a shadow quickly darken the small window in the front door. A moment later, the door was whipped open.

Stacie's father stood in front of Cole, looking more menacing than Cole had ever seen the man.

"How dare you come to my house?" Clark said from behind clenched teeth.

"Please, sir, just hear me out."

"Hear you out? Get off of my property!" Clark yelled, his chest heaving.

"But, sir, I . . . you . . . just—" Cole could barely get the words out before he was snatched by the front of his shirt.

"Get away from here right now, or, I swear, I'll do something I'll be sorry for," Clark said, before forcefully pushing Cole backward.

Cole stumbled, tripped, fell down the two steps behind him, and landed on his back. He looked up to see the door slamming shut.

Chapter Twenty-Six

HALF AN HOUR LATER, Cole was standing at Donesha's front door. She leaned out, wearing nothing but a thigh-length nightgown.

"I'm sorry to be coming over here so late," Cole said. "I been driving around for a couple of hours and didn't feel like going home. I just feel like talking. Can we do that?"

"Sure, Cole," Donesha said, opening the door to let him in.

Cole stepped into the dark living room and headed over toward the sofa.

"No, come up to my room," Donesha whispered.

"I don't think we—"

"My mother's in her room, but I don't think she's asleep yet," Donesha said, holding out a hand for Cole to take. "I don't want her saying anything about me having company this late. Just c'mon, Cole."

Cole wasn't in the mood to argue. He took Donesha's hand and allowed her to lead him up the stairs to her room.

Cole paused at the open door. The room was dark except for the glow from Donesha's portable stereo, which was playing soft, slow jams, and a night-light that was plugged in to one of her walls.

"I'll sit over here," Donesha said, taking a seat in the chair at her desk. "You can sit on my bed. But give me your jacket first."

Cole pulled his jacket off and handed it to Donesha. He sat on the bed and glanced at her out of the corner of his eye as she hung his jacket up in the closet. He quickly looked away before she turned around.

"I went over there," Cole said as Donesha sat back down. "I went to Stacie's house."

"You did what? Did you talk to her?" Donesha said, suddenly appearing very concerned.

"No. Her father came to the door, and I knew he'd be mad, but he was, like, crazy. He told me to get the hell away from his house; then he grabbed me and pushed me down the steps."

"Cole!" Donesha gasped. "Are you okay?"

"Yeah, but . . . but I needed to see Stacie today. I mean,

I really needed to see her, and she didn't call me or anything. Did you give her my letter?" Cole asked, finally looking up at Donesha.

"I gave it to her. She took it and left, so I don't know if she read it, but I gave it to her. Anyway, how's your father doing?"

It was helpful for Cole to talk to someone about his father, so he was thankful that Donesha had asked. "Not good," he replied. "He had a seizure while he was in his coma, and they don't know what happened. They don't know if he's going to wake up." Cole's voice was starting to crack, but he tried to keep himself together, not wanting to break down. "They don't even know if he's going to live." And then he felt a tear race down his cheek.

Before he knew it, Donesha was beside him on the edge of the bed, her hand on his arm.

"Cole, don't. Your father is going to wake up. Your father is going to be fine."

"But how do you know?"

"You're too sweet and kind a boy for something this bad to happen to," Donesha said, wiping his tears away.

"I went over to Stacie's house to talk to her about this," Cole said as he jumped up from the bed, getting angry. "I needed to talk to her; I needed her to be here for me, but she isn't. She never is. I can never call her; I can never see her when I want to. I have to always watch out for her damned father, because I don't know what the hell he's going to do.

I'm tired of it." Cole dropped himself back onto the bed. "Now I have to go through this alone."

"You're not alone, Cole," Donesha said.

"But what if my father dies?" Cole said, as more tears started to come.

"He won't die," Donesha said, putting her arms around him.

Cole did not try to push her away. He was thankful for the sympathy, for the compassion she offered. "But what if he does?"

Through the darkness, Donesha looked into Cole's eyes. She slowly leaned forward, softly kissed one of his wet cheeks, then the other. "Then I'll be here for you, regardless," she said, still looking into his eyes, moving closer to him.

A moment later, Cole felt Donesha's soft lips pressed against his. He did not pull back. When he felt her tongue trying to slip between his lips, he simply let it, and started to kiss her back.

Donesha gently leaned into Cole, pushing him backward onto the bed.

He still didn't stop her, and when she grabbed the bottom of his shirt and started to raise it over his head, Cole lifted his arms so she could.

Donesha straddled him, the sheer nightgown now hiked up over her hips. As she continued to kiss Cole, she grabbed both his hands, slid them down, and placed them on her bare behind.

That sent a jolt through Cole's entire body. He squeezed her tight, then thrust his hips up between her legs.

Donesha moaned and gyrated. Cole's head started swimming.

"I want you to take off your clothes," Donesha whispered in Cole's ear.

"I don't think I should," Cole whispered back.

"Okay, then," she said, lifting Cole's hands from her body. She rose up off him, pressing a hand down between his legs as she did, as if to confirm that he was as excited as she thought he was. Then she got off the bed and stood before him. "I will."

Donesha pulled the straps of the nightgown down off her shoulders and let the garment fall to her feet. There she stood, completely naked, her breasts firm and round, her stomach flat, her hips beautifully curved.

Cole stiffened more in his pants; he thought he might lose control of himself at that moment.

"How about now?" Donesha said.

Cole didn't say anything. He couldn't speak. When Donesha came toward him, he did not move an inch, did not even blink. And when she started to unbuckle his belt, pull down his zipper, and tug at his jeans and then his boxers, all Cole did was lift his hips and let Donesha slide his clothes down his legs.

He stared at her in near awe, his mouth hanging open, his breath coming harder.

Donesha reached over, slid her nightstand drawer open, and pulled something out of it.

It was a tiny packet. She stuck it between her teeth, tore it open with one hand, and, without saying a word to Cole, without even looking up at him, she grabbed him and rolled the condom on.

Cole threw his head back and shut his eyes, feeling more pleasure than he ever had.

"Are you ready for this?" Donesha said, her voice low and raspy.

"Yes," Cole almost cried.

Donesha pressed his knees together, straddled his thighs, and slowly, very carefully, slid down.

Chapter Twenty-Seven

IT WAS JUST AFTER midnight, and Stacie and Mya stood near the front door of Mya's apartment, trying not to make a sound as someone banged on the door.

"I know you're in there, Stacie. Just open the door so we can talk this over," Stacie heard her father say.

Mya silently mouthed the words *Let's hear what he has to say*, but Stacie shook her head, mouthing, *No!*

It was the second time that night their father had come knocking on Mya's door. The first time had been almost four hours earlier. He had seemed much angrier then, not appearing to want to discuss the situation, but, rather, telling Stacie to come home—or she'd be grounded for the rest of her life.

He'd left after twenty-five minutes of that. But now he was back.

"Stacie, open the door," Clark said again, but this time it sounded as though he were practically begging. Still, neither Mya nor Stacie said a word.

Stacie heard her father lean up against the door; she sensed his weight press against it, as though he were exhausted by the long ordeal.

There was silence for almost two minutes.

Mya mouthed the words *What's going on?*

Stacie just hunched her shoulders. She was about to say something aloud, thinking their father might have left, when Clark finally said in the softest voice, as if speaking to himself, "I don't want to lose you, Stacie. I've been far too overprotective. Instead of denying your feelings, I should've listened to them. I don't care that you slept with that boy. I would've rather you hadn't, but it's done now. We'll work through that if you just come home."

Aw, Mya mouthed, sarcastically wringing her fists in front of her eyes.

"And Mya, if you're listening, I apologize to you as well. Not having either of you around made me realize that being alone is far worse than proving some kind of point.

"Mya, you got pregnant when you were eighteen, and you were old enough to decide whether you wanted to have the child or not. You kept her, and I should've respected that. I guess I was so concerned with you abiding by my rules and the possibility of some other man taking you away from me, that I acted a damned fool, and ended up losing the love of my first daughter. Please forgive me, and come home. You're welcome to anytime, if you like."

Mya stood by the door, tears in her eyes now. She seemed as though she were about to turn the knob and let her father in, but Stacie quietly grabbed her hands and held them firmly.

No! Stacie mouthed. *No!*

Five minutes later, Stacie and Mya heard their father step away from the door and leave.

Afterward, Mya opened the door and peered out, just to make sure.

"Are you crazy?" Mya said, closing the door. "He wants both of us to come. I'm waking up Tiff, and we're getting out of here."

"No. He's just saying that because he's lonely."

"Whatever it takes for him to realize he was wrong," Mya said.

"And what happens when we get back there, and he's rummaging through both our closets for condoms?"

"He's learned his lesson, Stacie."

"He needs to learn it some more, before I go back there," Stacie said, lowering herself onto the living room sofa.

Mya sat down beside her. "You're going to have to talk

to him sooner or later. Tell him that you really didn't sleep with Cole."

"Why?"

"Because you didn't. You know it's ripping Dad up inside thinking it's true."

"So what?" Stacie said, getting defensive. "Are you on his side now? Even after how he's treated you, you don't feel he should be in any pain?"

"I'm not on his side," Mya said. "All I'm saying is, why have him mad at you for something that ain't even true. Trust me, I wouldn't have let him throw me out of the house, be living the way I've been living, if I didn't have a really good reason. I'm not saying to rush back to him and apologize right now, but don't be so quick to have him against you. It ain't as easy as you think it is. And we need to take advantage of his offer, before he takes it back."

The next morning, Stacie woke up in Mya's bed and yawned, stretching her arms over her head. She smelled eggs and bacon cooking, which was a good thing, because she was starving.

She pulled herself out of bed and headed toward the kitchen, wearing a pair of her sister's pajamas. "I'm glad you know how to cook, because I'm—"

She stopped, dumbstruck in the doorway to the kitchen. There at the table was her father, a plate set before him, as though he were about to eat breakfast with them.

Without a word of acknowledgment, Stacie walked past Mya at the stove, sidestepping Tiff in her baby chair and completely ignoring her father. She pulled a glass out of the cabinet, opened the fridge, and filled the glass with orange juice; then she headed back toward the door.

"Just wanted to get some orange juice before I left," she finally said over her shoulder to Mya.

"Wait, Stacie," Mya said. "Daddy has something to say to you."

"'Daddy'? He throws you out of the house, acts like he doesn't know you, and now he's 'Daddy' again? Why did you even call him?"

"I didn't," Mya said. "He never left. When I opened the door for the paper this morning, he was out there, sleeping."

"But last night—" Stacie said.

"I left to go to the bathroom, and it didn't seem like you two were going to let me in," Clark said, smiling a little.

"I don't care. I'm leaving," Stacie said, turning again to go.

"I told him you didn't sleep with Cole," Mya said. "I told him it was because you didn't want to go back on your word to him."

Stacie halted, then turned back around. "So? That doesn't change a thing. He still went through my things, and because I was keeping my word, I ended up losing my boyfriend."

"Stacie," Clark said, pushing back from the table and

{ 167 }

getting up, "I swear, I promise, really, honestly this time, that'll I'll never distrust you again. Just like you said, you're almost seventeen, and you'll be away at college in a couple years. To be frank, I don't want to waste that time trying to prove that you're telling me the truth or not. It's easier believing you."

"And what about Cole?" Stacie asked.

"He's a good kid. We'll all have a talk. I'm sure we can fix things between the two of you."

"And you won't be as strict with him? And he can come over when you're not there?"

Clark rolled his eyes and sighed heavily. "Yes. But that doesn't mean you don't have to be responsible. Besides, your big sister will be there to watch you when I'm not," Clark said, smiling at his older daughter.

Mya returned the smile.

"Now, if you don't mind, can you come over here and give your old man a hug so we can eat breakfast?"

Stacie walked over and wrapped her arms around her father, squeezing him tight. A second later, Mya joined them both, and the three of them stood in an embrace, none wanting to let go.

Chapter Twenty-Eight

THE NEXT DAY, after spending the better part of the afternoon at the hospital and receiving the good news that the seizure had not in any way negatively affected Franklin's chances of recovery, Cole and his mother sat outside in their backyard, talking.

They sat on the swing set that Cole had played on as a child.

"Ma," Cole said, digging with the toe of his shoe at the thinning grass, "did you ever regret kicking Pops out?"

"Every day," Lana said. "But I think I did it for a good reason, so I try not to let the guilt get to me."

"I did something last night that I regret," Cole admitted, "and I don't know if the reason was good enough to keep the guilt from getting to me."

Lana halted her slowly moving swing and turned to her son. "What did you do?" she asked.

"I lost my virginity last night."

Lana turned away, pursing her lips for a moment. Then she turned back to Cole. "You and Stacie finally did it, huh? I hope you were safe."

"I was safe, Ma. But it wasn't with Stacie. That's why I'm feeling guilty."

"Oh, Cole," Lana said, disappointment on her face. "What happened?"

Cole told his mother everything, about going to Stacie's house, the altercation with her father, and then going over to Donesha's.

"This is the little girl you used to go to the movies with in grammar school?"

"She ain't so little anymore."

"I'm sure," Lana said. "Do you have feelings for her?"

"She's a friend, but it's not like I love her."

"But you still love Stacie?"

"Yes, of course. I want to get back together with her, but I feel like there's no hope now. What do I do?"

"You tell Stacie everything that happened."

Cole laughed. "Yeah, right, Ma. 'Hey Stacie, I love you and miss you. Oh, yeah, and I slept with your best friend. So, can we get back together?' I can't do that."

"And what happens when she finds out?"

"She won't. Donesha said she'll keep it a secret. No one will know."

Chapter Twenty-Nine

THE NEXT MORNING, on his way to school, Cole noticed that his friends were abnormally quiet.

Cole had given them an update about his father, telling them that he was stable and that there was still a chance that he could pull out of his coma.

"Glad to hear that," Marc said.

"Cool," Drew said.

"He'll be fine," Tony said.

But none of them said much after that.

Cole was wondering what was going on when he heard whispering behind him.

He looked over his shoulder; Drew and Tony turned

away quickly, acting as though they hadn't said a word.

Cole ignored them and continued walking, but then he heard the whispering again, followed by muffled laughter.

He quickly spun around. "What the hell is going on?"

"What?" Tony said.

"Y'all ain't say a word all the way to school, and now you whispering and laughing like little girls. Let me in on the secret."

"Naw, big man," Marc said, resting his hands on Cole's shoulders and massaging him, as though Cole were a prize-fighter. "Why don't you let us in on *your* secret?"

"What secret? I don't have a secret."

"Really?" Drew said. "That's not what we heard, stud," he said, pushing his fist forward in a thrusting motion.

Cole's heart started to pound rapidly in his chest. There was no way that his boys could've known. "What the hell are you all talking about?"

"Jig is up, Cole," Marc said, bear-hugging his friend from behind. "The boy is no longer a virgin!" he practically yelled, continuing to hold him as Drew and Tony took turns playfully punching Cole in the chest, arms, and shoulders.

"Get off of me!" Cole shouted, struggling to escape.

"Why were you holding out, Cole?" Tony said.

"Yeah, when were you going to tell us?" Drew asked, still punching Cole.

"I said, get off of me!" Cole yelled much louder, his eyes burning with anger.

Marc let go of Cole, and Tony and Drew stopped punching him.

"How did you find out?" Cole asked, breathing heavily.

"You don't know?" Marc said.

"No," Cole said.

Marc shook his head. "Come with me."

In the school library, Marc sat down at one of the computers, where he pulled up a MySpace page and then stood up again to let Cole sit down. Cole saw that it was Donesha's page.

Cole read the page in shock.

It was covered with photos of him and Donesha. She must have gotten his photos from old school newspapers and yearbooks. There were so many of them that Cole suspected she had been collecting them for some time.

There was only one picture of them together. That was from his birthday party in the eighth grade. All the others had her image somehow superimposed onto his, making it look as if she were kissing his cheek, or as if they were walking arm in arm.

"Man, that girl got graphic-design skills," Tony said, leaning over Cole's shoulder.

Cole shot Tony an evil look.

The wallpaper for the page consisted of the words *Cole loves Donesha* repeated over and over, as if it had been written during punishment in detention.

Cole shook his head in disgust.

"That ain't all, man," Marc said. "Scroll down."

Further down the page, Cole saw a long block of text, the title of which screamed, in big, blinking, blue letters, *THE FIRST TIME I MADE LOVE TO COLE.*

He skimmed over it long enough to realize that it gave a description of the encounter in breathtaking detail.

Cole clicked the CLOSE WINDOW icon in the corner of the screen. "Who else knows about this?" Cole asked, getting out of his chair.

"Everybody she e-mailed," Drew said.

"How many people is that?" Cole said.

"However many people she got on her e-mail list," Tony said.

"Does Stacie know yet?" Cole asked.

Marc shrugged his shoulders. "I don't know. But if she don't, you better find her before Donesha does."

Chapter Thirty

MINUTES BEFORE the start of first period, Donesha watched from around the corner as Stacie pulled a book from her locker, closed it, then headed for class.

After updating her MySpace page the previous night, Donesha had sent e-mails out only to the boys on her list. She knew that if any girls in the school got wind of what had happened, it would have spread like an STD, and Stacie would have found out before Donesha had the chance to tell her. Donesha wanted to be there to see the look on Stacie's face when she found out.

Donesha carefully followed Stacie, ducking behind students and hiding behind corners, until Stacie stepped into the girls' bathroom.

Perfect, Donesha thought, walking right up to the door, where she waited a moment before stepping in herself.

Nobody else seemed to be in there. Only one stall door was closed.

Donesha stepped up to one of the four sinks and admired herself in the mirror. Her hair was pulled up to show off her neck, or, more specifically, what was on her neck—a huge, red hickey.

Cole hadn't put it there, but that didn't matter. That morning, Donesha had stood in front of her mirror and pinched her neck so long and so hard that it looked as though a vampire had been chomping on her. She wanted a dramatic visual effect when she told Stacie that she'd had sex with her man.

Stacie was happy that things had worked out with her dad and Mya the day before. She'd thought of calling Cole and telling him the good news about her father. But she had been having a very good time hanging out with her reunited family, and she was reluctant to do anything to detract from the huge strides they'd all just made together.

Besides, Stacie figured it would be much more fun to tell Cole her news in person, so that she could see his face light up when he found out that things were going to change.

As Stacie exited the stall, she imagined Cole throwing his arms around her, spinning her in the air, and kissing her.

She couldn't wait to see him. She grinned, feeling giddy.

Stepping out, she was surprised to see Donesha there fixing her hair in the mirror.

Stacie stepped up next to her, turned the faucet on, and started washing her hands. "Hey, Donesha."

"Hey, Stacie," Donesha said, turning completely around to face her. "How's it going? You read Cole's letter?"

"Yeah, I read it."

"What did it say? Was it a Dear Jane letter, like you thought?" Donesha asked, smirking.

Stacie didn't know what Donesha thought was so funny. She almost seemed eager to hear bad news from Stacie. "No. It was just some private stuff he wanted to tell me."

"You want to talk about it?" Donesha asked, tilting her head to the side.

"No. Like I said, private stuff. Thanks, though." Then Stacie caught sight of the massive red mark on Donesha's neck. "Damn, girl, what you do, burn yourself with a hot comb?" she joked.

Donesha waved her hand at Stacie. "Don't be stupid. It's a hickey."

"I'll say. Whoever's been sucking on you must've been frantic. He should slow down next time," Stacie said, turning and heading for the door.

"Why don't you tell your boy that?" Donesha said softly, but loud enough for Stacie to hear.

Stacie stopped just in front of the door.

"You know," Donesha said, admiring her hickey in the mirror again, "you really think you're something, don't you?"

"No," Stacie said, slowly walking back toward Donesha. "You said something about 'my boy.' Who were you talking about?"

"Who do you think I was talking about, Stacie?" Donesha said, turning away from the mirror to face Stacie. "When we dated, I would've given him anything in the world he wanted, including sex."

"He was twelve years old. He wasn't even thinking about sex when you two dated."

"But he's thinking about it now, and you ain't giving it to him."

Stacie looked at Donesha as if she didn't know what she was talking about. "I'm not having this discussion. I'm late for class."

"He's damned near a grown man, Stacie. He was starving for it. He had to get it from somewhere."

"What? What do you mean 'had to get it'?" Stacie said, starting to feel an uneasy queasiness in her belly.

"The hickey," Donesha said, lovingly running her fingers across it. "It was Cole. Saturday night, he came by your place, needing comfort, wanting to be with you. But you weren't there for him, so he came to me. And you better believe I gave him all the comfort he needed, and he gave it right back to me." Donesha's voice was full of venom.

"No. You're lying."

"If you could've felt him, girl. All that frustration of wanting you, fantasizing about you; he took it out on me. And he was so strong, and long, and hungry. Three times," Donesha said, holding up her fingers.

"You're lying," Stacie repeated, her voice starting to crack.

"Three times we did it that night. You know, I can't understand for the life of me why you ever turned that down."

"I don't believe you," Stacie insisted, wiping her sleeve across her eyes.

"No? Go to him. Ask him. If he says we didn't, he's lying."

"But . . . why? You're supposed to be my friend!"

"And you were supposed to be mine!" Donesha spat back. "You knew Cole and I used to date. But you dated him anyway. I loved him!"

"You were in middle school. How in love could you have been?" Stacie looked at Donesha, shaking her head, the tears falling freely now down her face. "I hate you for what you did. I hate you," she said, backing up to the door, pulling it open. "I hate you!"

"That's all right," Donesha said nonchalantly. "Because your man loves me."

Chapter Thirty-One

WITH FIVE MINUTES to go till the end of first period, Cole held his phone beneath his desk, typing in the message *Meet me @ gym after cls.* He pressed SEND, shooting the text off to Donesha.

After seeing Donesha's new MySpace page, Cole had hurried down the hallway toward her locker, trying to find her before class started.

He called her cell phone, but she did not pick up.

Then he texted her, asking her where she was, but he got no response that way, either.

Now, as the bell rang for the end of first period, Cole's phone vibrated in his hand.

He saw that it was a text from Donesha. He opened the message and read, *OK sweetheart!*

Cole snapped the phone closed, snatched his book off his desk, and bolted out of the classroom.

Pacing in front of the door to the gym, Cole kept looking up to see if Donesha were coming. He had practically run all the way there, trying his best not to bump into Stacie, not knowing whether or not she had found out what happened.

A moment later, Cole heard footsteps behind him. He whirled and saw Donesha approaching. He ran to her, grabbed her by the arm, and yanked her around the corner, out of sight of any students.

"Whoa, baby. You can have some more if you want. You don't have to be rough," Donesha said playfully. "Give me a kiss."

Cole looked at her as though she were insane. "What?"

"I said, give me a kiss. I've missed you since Saturday night."

"Are you crazy? What the hell have you done? E-mailing everyone, putting my pictures on your MySpace page, telling the whole damned world that we had sex? What is the matter with you?" He slapped his palm against the wall just beside Donesha's head.

"An expression of love, baby. If I'd known it would've made you this mad, I wouldn't have done it. But I can take it down. It's no big deal, Cole."

"That's right, you're going to take it down," Cole said, now right up in her face, his finger pointed at her barely an inch from her nose. "Right after you leave here. You're going to the library and taking that crap off."

"All right, all right, I'll take it down."

Cole calmed down slightly and took three steps away from Donesha. Then he turned back toward her again and said, "Did you tell her?"

"Tell who what?"

"Tell Stacie that we slept together?"

"Of course I told her."

"Why?" Cole yelled at the top of his lungs, his voice echoing down the corridor. He rubbed the sides of his head with his fingers and grimaced as though he were experiencing the worst migraine of his life. "Why in the hell did you have to tell her?"

"Because she needed to know. You two were broken up. You said that yourself. So what was I supposed to do? I'm her friend. I had to tell her that you and I were getting back together."

Cole spun around; Donesha was crazier than he had ever imagined. "We aren't getting back together. Are you stupid? What would even make you think something like that?"

Donesha's face fell. "I see. When you get bad news about your father, you come to my house, because you want someone to talk to, to comfort you. Then you have sex with me—and now you're asking me why I think we're getting back together?"

Cole paused for a moment, realizing how all of this must have looked from Donesha's point of view. But Donesha knew that he still loved Stacie; he had told her as much. She would have to have been blind and deaf not to have realized that.

"I don't care what you say," Cole said. "We are not back together. You were wrong for e-mailing everybody, wrong for putting our business out there like that, and especially wrong for telling Stacie what you did."

"What difference does it make to you?"

"Because I still love her, Donesha."

Donesha looked as if she had just been slapped in the face. "Don't say that, please."

"I still love her, and it don't matter, this nonsense you pulled. I'm going to get her back."

"She doesn't want you anymore."

Cole moved closer to Donesha and looked her in the eye. "To hell with you."

"I'm tellin' you. She doesn't want you."

"To hell with you!" Cole yelled again, backing away from Donesha. "Don't you ever come near either one of us again."

Cole turned and started running down the hall. He would go directly to Stacie's next class, hoping to catch her before she went in. But just as he was starting to run up the stairs, he heard his name spoken over the PA system.

"Cole Stevens, please report to the principal's office, ASAP. Cole Stevens, please report to the principal's office, ASAP."

He froze, halfway between the first and second floors. Stacie's class was just five doors down the hall on the next level, but something told Cole that the summons had something to do with his father.

He turned around and ran back down the stairs, heading for the principal's office.

Chapter Thirty-Two

Half AN HOUR LATER, Cole was rushing down the hospital corridor, checking each door number as he tried to find his father's new room.

When Cole had gotten to the principal's office, the assistant principal, Mrs. Gidry, told him that his mother had called from the hospital. His father had awakened and was looking for him.

Now, finding room number 764, Cole stepped in.

His mother was sitting on the side of the bed. Cole was surprised to see his father sitting up, clean-shaven in a crisp white hospital gown; he was smiling, looking healthier than he had looked in some time.

Cole wrapped his arms around his father's neck and held him tight. "We were so worried, Dad," he said, full of emotion.

"I know, son," Franklin said, hugging Cole back, rocking him gently.

After their hug, Cole gave his mother a kiss on the cheek and said, "I came as soon as I got your message."

She squeezed his hand and smiled. Then she moved from the bed to a chair. "You can sit here."

There was an awkward silence for a moment, as if none of them knew what to say—or were willing to say what they were thinking.

Then Cole finally spoke. "So, you're fine now?"

"That's what the doctor said, but I'm going to have to start rehab all over again, because of what I did."

"And why did you do what you did, Pops? You told me it had been almost six months. Why would you throw all that away?"

Franklin looked to Lana, as if for help. She looked back at him and said, "Tell him."

"I was ashamed, son."

"Of what?" Cole said.

"Of everything I did. Of everything I didn't do. Yeah, for the past six months, I was doing okay, working, going to class, staying off the drugs, but that man, your mother's fiancé—"

"Ex-fiancé," Lana interjected.

"—Made me aware of how weak I had been to leave you all in the first place."

"But you didn't leave. Ma threw you out."

"No, Cole. Don't do that," Franklin said. "Don't blame that on your mother. If I'd been the man I should've been, when she asked me to leave, I would have asked her if I could stay, under the condition that I get in a program. I didn't do that. I walked away and didn't come back to check on you, didn't give you guys any sort of help for two and a half years. That was unforgivable. Every day, I tried not to think about how I was neglecting you all, and then, one day, I didn't have to try. I just no longer thought about it. That is, until that man, Edric, laid it all out for me."

"That's why you tried to kill yourself?" Cole asked.

"That's not what I was trying to do. I was just depressed and feeling sorry for myself, so I did something I knew I shouldn't have. Kind of like when your mother gets depressed and eats a whole pint of Ben & Jerry's ice cream."

"It's not the same, thank you," Lana said. "And I don't do that anymore."

"Sorry," Franklin said, smiling. "So, that's what happened. But I just want to tell you and your mother that I'm sorry for scaring you two, and sorry for letting you down three years ago and leaving you alone like that."

"So does that mean you're coming home?" Cole said, getting hopeful.

Again, Franklin looked at Lana. This time, she looked away.

"Ma, can you let Pops come home with us?"

"Cole . . ." Lana said.

"Before this happened, he was clean for six months," Cole pleaded.

"Cole, stop. A lot has happened, and there's a lot to think about. I just don't know if this is the right time."

"We can talk about that later," Franklin said. "Besides, there's something more important we need to discuss."

"What's that?" Cole said.

"You, Cole. Your mother told me that you did something you probably shouldn't have, and you were hoping your girlfriend wouldn't find out about it."

"Yeah, that's right," Cole said, his head down.

"Did she find out?"

"Yeah."

"And what are you going to do?"

"Pops, I don't know," Cole said, rubbing his head with his fingers. "It's more messed up than you can believe. I love Stacie so much, but this is like the worst thing I could've ever done to her. After this, I know she's thinking that I don't love her anymore, that I never have. I mean, why would she think anything different? Things get a little hard, and I leave her. Take the easy way out to get what I want. How am I supposed to be able to fix that?" Cole had gotten up from the bed and was

{ 189 }

now pacing anxiously up and down the room, exasperated with himself.

"I think I might be able to help you."

"Uh-uh. You can't understand how bad a situation like this is."

"Really?" Franklin said. "Well, if I happened to be in a situation as horrible as yours, you know what I'd do?"

"What?" Cole asked, not expecting much from the advice his father was about to offer.

"I'd go to Stacie," Franklin said, looking at Lana, "and I'd say, I need to talk to you."

Cole listened to his father's story and realized that he was getting a live demonstration.

Looking at Cole, Franklin continued, "Then I'd say to Stacie—" He turned to Lana. "—I've loved you from the first time I saw you. From that moment, you were the woman I knew I wanted to spend the rest of my life with, and you made me the happiest man in the world by giving me the opportunity to do that. We had wonderful times together, and we loved each other, like I'm sure neither one of us ever thought we had the ability to. But we did it. And it was so good. But then at the first sign of trouble, the first sign of hardship, I must've forgotten how much your love meant to me. Because I left you. I let you go, and it was the worst decision I made in my life." Franklin wiped away a tear that had fallen from his eye. "But, baby, as sure as we are sitting here right now, I promise, if you just forgive me for my foolish mistakes, give me just one chance, I'll prove to you that I can love you that way again."

Cole looked at his mother's eyes and saw tears, and he knew that his father's words held special meaning for her.

"Take me back, baby. I miss you. I miss my son, my family," Franklin said, leaning in and kissing Lana on both cheeks. "Please, take me back."

Lana tried to speak through the sobs that were now coming fast and free. "I don't know what to say. . . ."

"Just say yes, Ma," Cole said.

"Just say yes, baby," Franklin said.

"Yes!" Lana cried, leaning in to embrace Franklin.

Chapter Thirty-Three

HOURS LATER, Cole stood again at Stacie's front door and rang the doorbell. He looked back at his car, but if her father told him to leave this time, Cole wasn't going to. He would be strong and say what he had to say to Stacie, just as his father had done with his mother earlier.

Then, just as before, a figure darkened the window in the door, and Cole braced himself for an icy reception.

The door opened, and Stacie's father appeared in the doorway—not menacing and furious as Cole had expected, but smiling. He held out a hand and said, "How are you, Cole?"

Cole hesitated for a moment before shaking the man's hand. "Fine, sir. How are you?"

"Good. I'm good. I assume you're here to see Stacie?"

"Yes, sir. I am."

"Not a problem," Cole was shocked to hear her father say. Mr. Winston put a hand on Cole's shoulder. "Before I let you in, I just want to apologize for getting physical with you like that the other day. Do you think you can forgive me?"

"Uh . . . yeah. Yeah, I can forgive you," Cole said, hoping it would be this easy to smooth things out with Stacie. Obviously, Stacie had not told her father about what had happened at school earlier. Cole figured that maybe that meant she'd had time to think about it and calm down.

"Good," Clark said. And with that, he stepped aside, saying, "Come on in."

Cole walked into the living room. He heard the front door close, and then Stacie's father was beside him, pointing up the stairs.

"First door on the right. If her door is closed, please knock before you enter."

"Go up there?" Cole said.

"Yeah. That's where her room is. First door on the right."

Cole wondered if this were some sort of game or trick, and whether, the moment he made it halfway up, Stacie's dad would drag him back down by his ankles and beat him to a pulp. He figured there was only one way to find out. He started up the stairs.

When he got to the second floor, he peered down from

around the corner, half expecting to see Stacie's father staring right back up at him. But there was no one down there.

Cole approached the first door on the right, inhaled, then knocked tentatively.

"Come in," Cole heard Stacie's soft voice say.

He pushed open the door. Stacie was on the bed, her back turned to him. She was pushing a box of tissues behind her pillow.

When she turned around and saw Cole, she immediately stood up and walked toward him. "No! No!" she said, pushing her hands into his chest, trying to force him out of the room. "Get out of here!"

"Shhhh!" Cole said, grabbing her arms and pushing the door closed with his hip. "Do you want your father to hear?"

"I don't care," Stacie said loudly.

"Then you don't want to hear what happened?" Cole whispered. "You want your father to throw me out of here and you never find out? Huh?"

Stacie fell silent. Cole felt her tense limbs soften a little in his grasp.

She pulled away from him, walked back to her bed, and sat down. "So, did you sleep with her?"

Cole swallowed hard. He didn't know telling the truth could be so difficult. "Yes," he admitted.

"Just get out," Stacie said.

"I'm not saying it makes it right, but you did break up with me."

"Because I thought not having sex with you would make you want to sleep with some other girl! I guess I was right. I just didn't think you'd do it with my friend."

"Stacie, even after you broke up with me, and after I tried to make up with you, you ignored me," Cole said.

"Make up with me how? By cursing me out in the hallway, in front of the entire school?"

"I apologized for that."

"When?" Stacie said.

"In the letter I had Donesha give to you."

"You didn't apologize to me in that letter—you dismissed me. Said you were going to find a woman to sleep with and told me not to ever call you again."

Cole looked astonished. "That's not what I wrote! I apologized! I told you how much I loved you."

"I have it right here," Stacie said, getting up and going to her desk. She pulled the crumpled letter out of a drawer and shoved it into Cole's hands.

Cole looked down at it, unable to comprehend what he saw. "I didn't write this."

"What do you mean?" Stacie asked.

"I mean, I didn't write this. My letter was three pages long, and said exactly the opposite of this one. Donesha must've rewritten it. I swear."

Stacie snatched the letter out of Cole's hands. "That bitch!"

"I tried a thousand times to get her to call you, and she kept telling me she couldn't reach you."

"That bitch!" Stacie repeated.

"And then the other night, I came by here looking for you. I wanted to share what was happening in my life with you. I needed to be with you, but you weren't here."

"So you went to be with her?" Stacie said.

"C'mon. I thought you didn't love me anymore. Every attempt I made to contact you failed. I thought you never wanted to talk to me again."

"So that makes it all right to sleep with her?"

"No, it doesn't make it all right. It didn't even mean anything. It just happened."

"Go, Cole," Stacie said, turning her back to him.

Cole thought about what his father had said to his mother; he tried to recall the words his father had used to win back his mother's heart. He had to make Stacie feel the same way.

"Baby," Cole said, "from the first day I met you, I loved you."

"Please, Cole," Stacie said, falling onto her bed and dropping her face into her hands, "just leave."

"Stacie, if you'd just give me another chance, I promise I won't—"

But before Cole could say another word, Stacie was up off her bed, walking past him.

"What are you doing?" Cole said.

Stacie opened her door and ran down the stairs.

Cole followed her, coming to a stop in the living room. He saw Stacie fling open the front door.

"Get out!" she screamed, tears streaming down her face, her eyes pink and puffy. "I don't ever want to see you again!"

Cole looked around. He saw her father enter the living room. From another hallway, Stacie's sister, Mya, walked in.

"What's going on?" Clark asked.

"Daddy, I want him out of here."

"Then you have to go, Cole," Clark replied, walking toward Cole as though he were about to snatch him up and toss him out like the last time.

"With all due respect, Sir, if you'd just hear me out," Cole said, backing away. "I did something wrong, but we all make mistakes. I just want to explain myself, and if Stacie doesn't want to forgive me after that, *then* I'll leave."

"I don't want to listen to a word he has to say, Daddy," Stacie said, though she seemed a little calmer now.

Clark looked at his daughter and then at Cole. Then he looked back at his daughter and said, "Would you mind if I did? Nobody knows about making mistakes like I do. Maybe it's worth just hearing his side. Don't you have feelings for him anymore?"

Stacie didn't answer right away. She looked at Cole, then looked away. "I still have feelings for him."

"Then let's hear what he has to say, shall we?" Clark turned to Cole and said, "What did you do?"

Cole hesitated, trying to swallow the lump in his throat. "I slept with another girl."

Cole saw the muscles in Stacie's father's jaw tighten.

"I see," Clark said. He shook his head, as though he couldn't believe what he was hearing. He walked over to Stacie and took her hand. "Close the door," he said.

Stacie obeyed; her father walked her over to the sofa and sat her down.

"This is a big decision, but I've learned my lesson about getting too much in your business, so it's your decision to make. Just let me say a few words first, and then I'll leave you two alone. I don't know all the circumstances regarding what's going on here, but you say you have feelings for Cole. And Cole there . . ."—Clark nodded over at Cole—". . . must have serious feelings for you, coming over here and risking his life by telling me what he just did. Now you can put him out, and never talk to him again, but if you say you love him . . . I don't know. It might be worth giving the man another chance."

"Thank you, Daddy," Stacie said, leaning forward and hugging her father.

Clark stood up and walked past Cole; he wrapped his arm around Mya's shoulder, and the two went out of the room, leaving Stacie and Cole alone.

Cole remained standing in the same spot near the door, as if waiting for permission to move.

Stacie sat still, looking stoic. Then she said, "Cole, could you come over here?"

Cole walked over and stood before Stacie.

"When I told you I thought we should break up, I regretted it the minute I said it," Stacie said, not looking up, but at the floor. "And knowing you weren't in my life anymore, I felt like I had lost my best friend. I would've given anything to have you back, because I was hurting. I guess I realized then how much I loved you. But I was wrong. Finding out you slept with Donesha made me feel like I was dying. That's when I really knew how much I loved you," Stacie said, now looking up at Cole. "Because if I hadn't, I wouldn't have felt anything. My father is right about everybody making mistakes, and he should know. He made a mistake that ruined an entire year of our family's life. I don't want this mistake to ruin any of our time, Cole."

Stacie stood up and took a step closer to him. She placed her hands in his and said, "Just promise me that this will never happen again. Because even though I'll always love you, I'll never speak to you again if it does. Okay?"

"Okay," Cole said, a smile of relief emerging on his lips. "I think I can do that." He pulled Stacie into a tight embrace, so thankful for her forgiveness that he never wanted to let her go.